ROGUE--ALIEN WARRIOR ACADEMY #1

TANA STONE

Broadmoor Books

CHAPTER ONE

Brooke

"Arrival at Lokar in T-minus-twenty." The computerized female voice announces, jerking me back to reality.

The metal floor of the shuttle shakes as we descend, and I clutch the cross-body straps holding me to the hard, bench seat. The blonde beside me has her eyes closed and her arms folded across her chest, and doesn't seem to even notice that we're landing. I consider nudging her, then decide against it. I can hear my father's gravelly voice in my head telling me to mind my business. As much as I hope I will not hear my father's voice bossing me around while I'm light years away from him, I listen to the advice and twist my head back to face front.

I look across to the bench seat on the opposite side of the shuttle and notice that the other cadets seem equally relaxed about our arrival. Some of the wide-shouldered men—mostly Army Rangers and Navy SEALs, with a few Marines and Air

Force pilots mixed in—are sitting tall with their hands resting on their legs. A couple of short-haired women with impressively broad shoulders themselves stare straight ahead. I drop my hands from the safety straps to my cargo pants and wipe my sweaty palms as casually as possible.

I'm way too nervous to sleep or even rest my eyes. This is my first trip off Earth—actually, the only time I've ever left the U.S., and one of only a handful of times I've been outside of Texas—and I'm about to be one of the first humans to set foot on an inhabited alien planet. My stomach does another somersault, and I try to swallow, even though my throat is thick.

The shuttle rumbles, and I smell burning fuel as the thrusters engage to steady our landing, a surprisingly comforting scent, and one I breathe in eagerly. After growing up in my father's mechanic shop, it's a smell that reminds me of home, and right now, I could use something familiar.

The shuttle touches down with a hard jolt, making my teeth rattle. I relax my hands and wipe them again on my pants.

"You okay?" The woman on the other side of me asks, as she starts to unfasten her straps.

I glance at her quickly before unhooking my own harness. "I'm glad we're finally here."

"Right?" She flips her long, brown hair off her shoulder. "Even at warp whatever, I feel like we've been traveling to Lokar forever."

"Same." I know what she means. When you're told you're going to travel in a high-tech alien spaceship at warp speed, you don't expect the trip to still take a week. At least the Lokarian ship had been bigger than the shuttle that's transporting us to the planet's surface.

"I'm glad we didn't have to make the trip in this thing." She peers around the compact, metal interior of the shuttle. "It's like being inside a tin can."

"Totally." I grin at her, but don't say anything else. I've never had female friends, so girl chat doesn't come naturally to me. She seems nice, though, and I remember seeing her on the Lokarian ship during the voyage. Like me, she's not one of the bulky soldiers, and I wonder what her specialty is.

If you're on board this shuttle, that means you're one of the best Earth has of something. Only the top soldiers, pilots, hackers, snipers, and spies have been chosen to enter the Lokarian Warrior Academy—the first such exchange between Earth and the alien race.

I'm still reeling from being chosen. Who knew being the fastest racer on the hoverbike circuit would have caught the attention of the U.S. Military and then the Earth Defense Corps? I didn't even know our military used hover bikes until the recruiters had shown up at my father's garage. I'd been sure they would have wanted one of my older brothers instead of me —they were definitely bigger and more badass—but they claimed my size would be an asset for the new bikes they were developing. It's the first time being barely over five feet tall has ever been a good thing for me.

I stand and stretch as everyone around me also unhooks and starts gathering their things. The throaty rumble of the shuttle engines has been replaced by the chatter of voices, as it seems to hit everyone that we're finally here. The eager conversation and occasional burst of laughter makes my nerves seem to dissolve, and I remind myself how lucky I am to be chosen for this inaugural class.

According to our top brass, the Lokarians have superior military technology and training, so being allowed to learn from their instructors at their top academy is more than an honor. It's a once-in-a-lifetime opportunity. One that we've all be warned severely not to blow.

I blow out another breath and reach overhead to grab my

duffel, standing on my tiptoes. A guy with a buzz cut and at least a foot on me tugs it off the top rack without me asking, winking at me and making me want to knee him in the balls.

"I feel that." The brunette I'd been talking to laughs, hooking her own duffel over her shoulder.

I realize I must not be hiding my irritation well, so I try to wipe the frown off my face. "What?"

Her hazel eyes sparkle. "I take it you're not a soldier, either."

I eye her quickly. She doesn't have the physique of a fighter. "I ride hoverbikes."

Her eyebrows rise, and she gives me an appreciative nod. "Well, that's more butch than what I do." She leans closer and lowers her voice. "I'm a hacker."

I cock my head at her. She doesn't look like any hacker I've ever seen.

"I know. I know." She flutters a hand at me. "I should be pale and pasty and about forty pounds overweight because I live in my mother's basement, right?"

I open my mouth to protest, but that *had* been exactly what I'd been thinking.

She nudges me and laughs again. "Don't feel bad. That's what everyone thinks." She holds out a hand. "My name is Autumn, by the way."

I shake her hand. "Brooke."

"Brooke the biker," Autumn says. "I like that."

I want to tell her that I'm not *that* kind of biker. I don't wear leather or ride vintage Harleys. The hoverbikes I ride leave those ancient machines in the dust. They're sleek, maneuverable, and fast as hell—precisely why the military has started using them in ground assaults.

I hoist my duffel onto my shoulder. "I guess I still don't get why they want people like us to go through an alien military academy. I mean, I race bikes. You hack. Most of these classes won't have anything to do with what we do."

Autumn shrugs. "I guess everything has changed, right? If we're going to be fighting against the Skrum, I guess we need to be prepared for anything."

I resist the urge to shiver at the mention of the Skrum. They're the real reason we're on Lokar.

An insect-like race of aliens that attacks like a swarm—decimating their enemies with their mass of ships and hive-like movements—they are a scourge upon the galaxy. A scourge Earth was not aware of until they set their sights on our planet and the Lokarians stepped in to save us.

We hadn't been aware of Lokar, either, but when the huge aliens arrived to warn us of the impending attack, our governments quickly accepted them as allies. The Skrum was prevented from reaching Earth, but the Lokarians warned us that we needed to be better armed and prepared for more attacks. The Skrum require massive amounts of water for their swarm, and Earth has enough water to keep them replenished for a considerable amount of time. All the more reason they can never be allowed to reach Earth, and why they will keep coming.

The guy who'd grabbed my bag looks over his shoulder at us. "I don't know about you, but I can't wait to kick some Skrum ass. Right, Red?"

I stare at him until Autumn elbows me. "I think you're Red."

My brown hair has some natural streaks of red in it, and on a very sunny day it might be called reddish, but no one has ever called me Red before. Fuck, I really want to knee this guy in the balls. If one of my brothers had called me Red, he would have already been clutching his nuts.

Instead of answering him, I give him a pointed look and motion with my head that he should keep moving forward, since him stopping to interrupt our conversation has left a gap in the line to get off the shuttle. His grin falters, but he walks forward.

Glancing back to make sure I haven't left anything behind, I see that the woman with long, white-blonde hair hasn't moved, and her eyes are still closed.

I exchange a look with Autumn, who shrugs and calls over me. "Hey, Sleeping Beauty."

The woman jerks awake, her eyes focusing on both of us and then the emptying shuttle. "Fuck me, are we already here?"

She pulls down her bag and follows us down the ramp, muttering a few more curses as our boots rattle the metal. The cursing quiets when we get outside and our feet hit the ground. I think we're all too busy staring to say anything.

I don't know what I expected Lokar to look like, but it takes me a moment to take it all in. We've set down on an open-air landing pad that's surrounded by a range of jagged black mountains that appear to be made of glossy rock and remind me of mineral formations as they jut up from the ground with sharp edges and points. The sun sits low in the white sky, small and dark red. The air is cool with a slight metallic tang to it, but it's breathable.

"Is that the academy?" Autumn asks, pointing to the massive structure silhouetted in front of the obsidian mountains.

"Has to be." A thrill goes through me at the sight of it. If I'd ever imagined what an alien academy would look like, this would be it.

Clear domes dot the expansive campus with tall, white spires stretching into the sky. Cylindrical buildings are covered in mirrored tiles, glinting in the light. Everything about the academy is sleek and modern, including the glimmering, holographic gates that we pass through as we follow the others up a path paved with matte, silver stones.

As each person walks through the iridescent light that appears to be a solid gate, the image flickers and hums, then the finials at the top of the gate posts glow green.

"What do you think that means?" I ask, twisting my head to look back after we've successfully gone through.

Autumn's eyes are wide. "I think it's some sort of biometric scan. If we weren't allowed in, I'm guessing the light wouldn't turn green."

So, the Lokarians have already sent our biometric information to the academy. I find this both cool and creepy.

After walking through the gates, we stop in front of a large building with a huge, steel arch extending out of the front to create a sort of space-age awning. Unfamiliar symbols are etched into the metal, and I'm pretty sure it identifies it as the Lokarian Warrior Academy, but in the Lokarian alphabet, which I can't read. It towers at least three stories above us, and is impressive as hell.

Even though all of us Earth cadets have been given universal translator implants so we can understand what the Lokarians say—and the aliens already have the devices implanted since we aren't the first alien race they've encountered—that doesn't mean I can read their language. Still, I'm fascinated by the foreign letters etched into the metal.

I drop my gaze to the group of aliens standing on the gleaming, white steps of the building, and my breath catches in my throat. I recognize the bronze skin and massive bulk. Lokarian males.

I take in the black uniforms that seem to conform to their broad muscles and impressive height. Gold Lokarian crests are stitched on the top right of the jacket, the design like double flames inside a ring. The pants—which are snug enough everywhere to make me do a double take and then try to avert my eyes—are tapered into heavy-duty, black boots.

Every one of the Lokarian males is well over six feet tall, with dark hair hanging around their shoulders and is standing ramrod straight. Correction, Lokarian military officers.

"Welcome to the Lokarian Warrior Academy, humans," the

Lokarian with long, nearly black hair shot with silver says without smiling. Then they all turn sharply on their heels and walk through wide, glass doors that seem to dematerialize as they pass through.

I steady my breath as we follow them inside. I'm definitely not in Texas anymore.

CHAPTER TWO

Koran

I'm standing alone on one of the transparent walkways that crisscross the towering entrance hall of the academy when the human cadets walk inside. They stare up at the clear ceiling that soars into the air, and the many curving walkways that bisect it.

I almost feel sympathy for the aliens, some of whom are gaping at the web of steel and glass within the massive dome, but I remember being just as impressed when I'd first walked into the hall only a few moons ago. Impressed by the modern grandeur of the top military academy on my planet, and hopeful that this would be the first step in a new life. That was before I knew what it would be like to be an outsider in the Academy.

I lean my forearms on the railing and peer down to get a better look at the new recruits, some who will be my students in the coming days. There are many males who are muscular and serious, as I expected, but there are also several females. This surprises me. Few Lokarian females attend our academy.

I can't help letting out a sound of derision as I assess these human females. They do not appear to be large, or particularly fierce. I cannot imagine them going into battle next to huge Lokarian warriors. Then again, I do not know much about humans. Perhaps their females are more deadly than they appear.

A group of Lokarian cadets stand a few metrons away from me, also looking intently below. I recognize three from my advanced class—males from the Kurvak clan who wear adornments on their wrists and arms. I tamp down my annoyance at this display, and remind myself that each of my planet's four clans has its own way of distinguishing itself. However, even if I can ignore the jewelry, I cannot ignore what the loudest one is saying to his friends.

"That one, there." He points to the humans below. "The one with long, pale hair."

The Kurvak cadet next to him laughs. "I would not mind riding her."

"Not if I claim her first."

The three males laugh, and then another lets out a low whistle "What about the small one with the hair pulled up?"

I follow their gaze and see the female they are talking about. She is small, her frame slight even next to the other human females, but she stands with her shoulders squared as she looks around. I wonder what such a tiny creature could excel at that would earn her a place as a cadet at the Lokarian Warrior Academy.

She glances up, as if she's heard the males talking, but her eyes move quickly over them and linger on me for a moment before she turns her attention back to the building's interior. Something about her gaze when it skirted over me makes my ire ignite as I listen to the Lokarian cadets laugh about passing her around.

"I'd be afraid of splitting her in half. Human cocks must be small, if these females can take them."

More laughter.

I pivot toward them. "Nothing better to do than ogle the new recruits?"

The cadets stop, looking over at me. They start to straighten into a salute then realize that I'm not wearing a military uniform.

I lock eyes with the Kurvak with the most disdainful expression on his face. "I would think you might want to spend some extra time on the pod track."

His bronze cheeks flame, but he clenches his jaw and mutters something under his breath about not having use for pods when he is a Lokarian senator like his father. It is not loud enough to be a rebuke, but I hear it, nonetheless.

"I hope I do not hear you disrespecting your fellow cadets again." My gaze shifts to each of them. "I would hate for *that* to get back to the Lokarian Senate."

They mumble some halfhearted apologies as they move away from me, no doubt to continue their commentary out of earshot.

I swivel my gaze back to the humans, but I do not see the small female. The group seems to be breaking into smaller clusters, and I suspect they will be shown their quarters and given orientation tours around the spacious campus.

I let out a relieved breath. I doubt I'll see her often. A human that small must be a medic or tech specialist. Even though she'll be required to attend my class for basic competence, she will move on quickly. I suspect all the human females will, which I welcome. I do not have time for distractions on my track. And it's clear the females are already a distraction.

I wonder if it will be different for the humans at the academy. They will be outsiders, as well, but maybe the Lokarians will accept a different species more than they will accept a member of the Vratvos clan like me.

I scrape a hand across my short beard. If I wanted to blend in and pretend I am not from the Vratvos, I would shave the scruff off my face. I glance down at my bare forearms. I would also do a better job of hiding the tribal marks that cover most of my upper body—the thick, gold swirls a mark of my clan.

I had tried to adapt when I'd first arrived, wearing my hair slicked back and covering my tattoos with long sleeves. It had fooled no one. I cannot outrun the suspicion and wariness the other instructors feel at having a member of the Vratvos as a guest instructor.

I straighten as a pair of fellow instructors pass by me, giving curt nods in my direction. I return their cool nods. As much as I had hoped to fit in at the academy, I have learned that I am not one of them. Not really. I am from Lokar, but I am also Vratvos, and I will always be considered Vratvos—an outsider. The roughest of the clans. The one that survives by our wits and sometimes by our crimes. The pod riders who earn gold marks on their bodies for each victorious fight or kill. The story of my life is etched across my body in tattoos and scars. There is no point in pretending to be something I am not, although sometimes I wish I could wipe away every bit of gold glittering on my skin.

"Koran."

The sharp voice makes me turn abruptly, but my shoulders relax when I see that it is Commander Daryx, the head of the academy. Although he could never be considered effusive, the Lokarian has been fair and welcoming to me—almost the only one who has. I also know it was him who requested my presence here, although I do not yet know why.

I incline my head at him as a sign of respect. "Commander Daryx."

He nods, the silvery braid on one side of his head swinging

forward, and cuts his eyes to the humans who are now being led out of the spacious entry hall. "You are no doubt aware of our recruits from Earth."

"Yes, sir." I hesitate. "These are the best the planet has for us?"

He frowns, his brows furrowing. "They have skills that may not be apparent at first glance. And if we are going to keep their planet out of Skrum hands, then we need to make sure they are trained as well as we can train them."

"Understood." I have no intention of going easy on the new cadets just because they are not Lokarian. I know what is at stake in the ongoing war against the Skrum. It's why my clan agreed to give up one of their top soldiers so I could come to the academy in the first place. If there is one thing that can unite the clans on my planet, it's a common enemy. And the Skrum are a very real and very deadly enemy.

The corners of his mouth twitch up. "There is one new recruit who is particularly skilled in your area of expertise."

I cock an eyebrow at him. "I did not know humans had pods."

"They call them hoverbikes. Similar to the motorcycles that used to be popular on their planet before hover propulsion was discovered."

I perk at this. I had not expected that these Earth recruits might bring me any qualified proteges. I rock back on my heels. "So, this cadet is skilled on hoverbikes? Riding or building?"

"From what I understand, both." He studies my face before continuing. "Brooke was one of the top racers on their hover-bike circuit before being recruited into the military."

I can't help grinning. A racer. No one at the academy can ride like I can—pods are the almost exclusive domain of the Vratvos—and I am eager for some competition again. "I look forward to instructing him, sir."

Commander Daryx's mouth widens into an actual smile. "Not him. Her."

I blink at him a few times. "I'm sorry, sir. Did you say 'her'?"

"Correct. Brooke is her first name, and she is very much a her." He spins on his heel—I suspect before he started laughing—and strides away from me, calling out over his shoulder. "Keep me posted on your progress, Koran."

I curse under my breath as I stalk off in the other direction. A female pod racer—or hoverbike, as they apparently call them on Earth? Is she crazy? Pods are lightning fast, hard to control, and incredibly temperamental. I know massive males who've almost broken their necks falling off a flying pod. And this human female is a racer?

I shake my head, muttering to myself as I head toward my quarters. The last thing I need is to worry about a human female splattering herself all over my track.

I ball my hands into fists. Great. Just *vlakking* great.

CHAPTER THREE

Brooke

I flop down on the narrow bed, flinching as I hit the stiff mattress. The room isn't much more inviting than the bed, I think, as I twist my head to take in the utilitarian space with white walls, a built-in wardrobe with flat-panel doors, and a desk that juts out from the wall over a single, straight-backed chair. Everything is stark white with sharp edges. Even the covering over the bed is tucked in so tightly I'm sure I could bounce a quarter off it. There's a sharp scent that I can't quite place, but I get the sense that this place has been seriously scrubbed down.

I'm tired after the flight and the seemingly endless tour around the academy campus, but I know I shouldn't be holed up in my room already. The faint rise and fall of the other women in my suite talking drifts in from the central living area, and force myself to sit up. I may not have grown up around other females, but if I'm going to survive at this alien academy, I know I need to make friends.

So far, the other military guys from Earth don't look promising, and the huge Lokarians scare me a little. They're too intense and controlled. The men I'm used to are rougher and looser and know how to take a joke. These alien warriors don't strike me as the type who've ever cracked a smile in their lives. I think about the one who'd welcomed us, with the silver streaks in his hair and the stern expression on his face, and I shiver.

"Come on, Brooke," I whisper to myself as I stand. "Time to learn how to talk to girls."

When I walk out of my room and into the main room of the quad suite, the other women are sprawled out on the boxy, white furniture.

I was pleased when I'd discovered that Autumn, the woman I'd met in the shuttle, was assigned the same suite, and I grin as I see her adjusting herself on a chair with chrome arms that appears to rock when you lean back.

"Any chance that's more comfortable than the beds?" I ask.

She looks up and laughs. "Nope. These Lokarians aren't into comfort, are they?"

The woman with pale hair who'd slept through the shuttle ride to the planet shrugs from where she sits on the couch. "It's better than any barracks I've ever been in."

I don't want to admit that my experience with military barracks on Earth is pretty minimal, since I was recruited almost immediately after our treaty with the Lokarians and rushed through an abbreviated version of basic training so I could be sent here. I'm guessing the rest of the women—like the men—are experienced soldiers with lots of deployments under their belts. The blonde sure looks like it.

"I'm Layla, by the way." She flicks her gaze first to Autumn, and then to me.

We both introduce ourselves, but no one makes a move to shake hands, so I sit down in the chair across from Layla and try to look as cool as she does with her arms stretched across the back of the couch and one leg crossed over the other at the knee.

"At least there's more than one shower in there." A fourth woman with a raven-colored braid down her back emerges from one of the doorways off the main room. "But you can tell they're not used to female soldiers, because there are no doors or curtains." She smiles and her gray eyes sparkle. "We're all going to get to know each other *very* well."

My stomach tightens. Just great. My first time living with women and it's already turning into some sort of schoolboy fantasy scenario. I must make some sort of groaning noise, because the other women all swivel their heads to me in surprise and then burst out laughing.

"What?" My face heats.

"Sounds like you really don't want to shower with us." The woman with the braid takes the other end of Layla's couch. "Don't worry. I won't take it personall,...?" She lets her sentence trail off as a question.

"Brooke," I say.

She inclines her head at me. "Elena."

Layla sits up and leans her elbows on her knees. "So, what's your story, Red?"

I frown at the nickname, then something hits me. "You weren't actually asleep on the shuttle, were you?"

She winks at me. "I just didn't want to have to talk to some of those cocky assholes. I know their type."

"Anyone you've served with before on this mission?" Autumn asks.

Layla shakes her head. "No, but I've known enough like them." She focuses her gaze on me again. "But you haven't, have you?"

"Military guys? No," I admit. "But I've known plenty of guys who think they're hot shit."

"Haven't we all, girl?" Elena flips her dark braid forward and brushes the end over the back of her hand.

"So, the military recruited you because you can ride hover-bikes?" Layla asks, her green eyes intense as she studies me.

Elena cocks her head as she looks me up and down. "Hover-bikes? I wouldn't have guessed."

I try not to bristle at this. "Yep. Race and build. What about you?"

The woman's expression shutters. "I'm career military. Like Layla."

Vague, but it doesn't look like she wants to share anything more. Layla glances at her but doesn't say anything, either.

"What do we think about these Lokarians?" Autumn asks, after a few more long seconds of silence. "They make our guys look like pussycats."

Layla lets out a breath. "Just because they're bigger than humans doesn't mean they're better warriors. Size isn't everything."

"I don't know if I agree with that." Elena's grin widens. "It may not be everything, but it sure as fuck is *something*."

Everyone laughs and exchanges knowing smiles, and my face flushes again. This is exactly why I avoid girl talk. It always gets around to sex, and eventually it comes out that I have almost zero experience. Then everyone freaks out that I'm almost twenty-three and have never gotten laid and becomes determined to find me the perfect first guy to fuck and it goes downhill from there.

It's not that I don't want to get laid, but when you're raised by a tough dad and three older, overprotective brothers who race bikes and run a garage, it's not so easy. My brothers made it their life's mission to chase off any guy who came sniffing around, and pretty soon no one in their right mind would so much as look at me, for fear of getting the shit kicked out of them.

It wasn't all bad, though. My brothers did teach me how to stick up for myself and fight, which I'm grateful for, considering how petite I am. At least no one here knows that they used to call me "Chi" for chihuahua because they said I was small but scrappy—and really annoying. Strangely, a lump forms in my throat as I think about my asshole older brothers and how much I suddenly miss their constant teasing.

"So, did you?"

I jerk my head up when I realize that Autumn has asked me a question, and I have no idea what it's about. "Sorry, what?"

"Did you see that some of the Lokarians have tattoos, but they're silver or gold and they shimmer?"

I shake my head. How did I miss that?

"Most of them cover them up with their uniforms," Elena says, "but I saw one with full arms in gold. It's pretty hot."

Layla drags a hand through her straight hair. "It's a clan thing. They mean something different to each group."

I remember reading about the Lokarians and their clan system, but I hadn't retained the names of the various groups, or what it all meant. There had been too much information to jam in my brain before leaving, and I'd focused more on the basics about their planet. Knowing that I'd be able to breathe the air had seemed more crucial than Lokarian politics.

"I guess we'll find out more tomorrow when we start meeting all our instructors." Autumn bites the corner of her lip. "You don't think they can kick us out on the first day, do you?"

Elena furrows her brow as she looks at her. "Why would they kick you out?"

"I'm not a badass like you all." She waves a hand at us. "I'm a hacker. I suck at weapons and combat, and anything that doesn't involve outsmarting a computer."

"Well, I'm a foot shorter than everyone else here." I sit

forward in the uncomfortable chair. "Two feet shorter, if you count the Lokarians. They didn't recruit us because we can beat up guys bigger than us."

"But we still have to go through the basic classes." Autumn holds up a tablet resting on a side table. "Fudge nuggets! Tomorrow I have weapons and hand-to-hand combat."

Layla's eyebrows pop up. "Fudge nuggets?"

"I think she means…" Elena says, in a stage whisper. "Actually, I don't know what the fuck that means."

"Don't worry," I tell her, ignoring Layla shaking her head. "We can all help you."

"That's right." Elena nods. "We girls have to stick together."

Layla lets out a breath. "First lesson. Do *not* say fudge nuggets."

CHAPTER FOUR

Koran

The first day with the new human recruits goes well. As well as can be expected, considering most of the humans have never ridden a space pod. Since Earth has sent their biggest and baddest soldiers, almost all of them are proficient on hover-bikes, but none impress me with exceptional skill or speed.

The humans wear dark-blue uniforms, instead of the black that our Lokarian cadets do, and none of them have long hair or braids, or anything but closely cropped hair. Except the females, that is, but there are few of them. I spot the occasional tattoo, but no human is marked like I am, and as far as I know, they do not have clans to distinguish them from one another. They do have various shades of skin, but my research has told me that Earthlings do not use this to differentiate anymore, although they used to in their dark and violent past.

I push aside thoughts of the alien planet as I stalk the length of the glass-domed garage, the chains on my boots jangling as I watch them practice mounting and dismounting. I note which of the humans is quickest and will move up to a more advanced class, and which will move quickly out of my area and on to something they excel in.

Pods are not for everyone, and they are more compact and maneuverable than the human hoverbikes, which also makes them harder to perfect. In military battles, they are essential for moving over alien terrain quickly, and getting into areas the smallest fighters can't reach. Fleets of pod riders are the ones sent into mountainous regions, or even jungles that sensors can't explore properly. It's one of the reasons my clan embraced them. They are also excellent for getting in and out of areas after doing something for which you don't want to get caught. I shake off thoughts of Vratvos and remind myself that at the academy, I am Lokarian first.

"Again," I bellow, after watching a particularly muscular human run and overshoot the seat of the bike and slip off. It takes more than big biceps to be skilled on pods, something most males fail to realize.

There are sighs and grunts, but they do it again, as I clasp my hands behind my back and rock back on my heels. I scan the wide-open space, and the rows of shiny white pods lined up and held in place by magnetic braces so that it appears each pod is hovering between two arched metal posts that hum as they keep the machines steady.

I know the cadets are impatient to race, or even engage the ignition, but I am firm in my belief that you cannot run before you walk. I narrow my eyes and study their gait as they race to the pods and leap on, breathing in the scent of fuel that permeates the garage. Even though it makes me lightheaded after inhaling it all day, I've always found the scent both comforting and intoxicating.

I stop and incline my head at a human who isn't as bulky as some of the others. "You. What's your name?"

He pauses and straightens. "Carter, sir."

The human has light-brown hair cut short. He isn't as tall as me—then, again, none of the humans are—but he's lean, with sinewy arms and rippled stomach muscles I can see through the damp sweat of his T-shirt. A good build for racing pods.

"What's your division?"

He furrows his brow as he looks at me. "Division?"

"Are you with the Wavy or the...?" I hesitate as I try to recall the human military terms.

The corner of his mouth twitches briefly. "You mean what branch of the military am I? I'm with the Navy. Naval intelligence."

Navy. That was it. The word still makes no sense to me, but I nod and cut my eyes to the pod he's been easily mounting. "Have you ever ridden before?"

"A hoverbike was my first vehicle back home."

"I'd like to move you up a class, Carter," I tell him. "That work for you?"

He seems surprised, and I suspect the military intelligence officer hadn't expected to be singled out in the pod class. Some of the other males shoot dark glances at him, no doubt wondering why their oversized arms aren't impressing me.

I step back and point to a handful of other humans. "Now, I'd like to see you do a running mount and engage your engines." I gesture to Carter with my head. "You, too."

I study the males, quickly assessing them and reassuring myself that I was right to single out Carter. He's fast and graceful, with sharp instincts. When the others are jolted by the engine roaring to life between their legs, he doesn't flinch. Of all my cadet classes of the morning, he's the one who stands out, and who I'd be comfortable adding to a Lokarian pod fleet.

Before I can tell the cadets to do the drill again, there is a loud buzz. The class period is over. Most of the humans look relieved, and a few rub their backsides as they make their way across the length of the garage toward the main academy building. I tell myself to go easy on the next group, but then change my mind when I realize that the next class is for advanced riders.

"Finally," I mutter to myself, rubbing my callused hands together. I'm itching to get some cadets out on the racing course today, and the Lokarians in my next group know how to ride.

Walking down the row of pods, I enjoy a moment of quiet between the classes after one group has left and before the other arrives. It doesn't last long. Soon, the Lokarians are striding into the wide-open space and taking their place at their usual pod. I greet most of them with silent nods, noticing that the cocky cadet from clan Kurvak is staring with his lip curled at the double doors behind me. I want to tell him to wipe the smirk off his arrogant face, but I hold my tongue. No need to antagonize my students. Not yet.

"Sir."

The soft voice makes me turn quickly and look down at the slight female. Her brown hair is pulled up and glints red in the sunlight slatting through the clear, domed roof. She wears the dark cadet training uniform, the pants snug on her slim legs and the dark T-shirt stretched shamelessly around her high breasts. Although her arms hang straight by her sides, I see the tension twitch at her mouth. A mouth that is full, with soft, pink lips that make me forget that she has addressed me.

Her blue eyes meet mine. "Cadet Butler, sir. Which pod would you like me to take?"

I take in her small stature and remember that Daryx told me about a human hover bike rider. "Brooke?"

Her face relaxes slightly, and she cocks her head to one side. "That's right."

I hate how much I like the sound of her name on my lips, and I cannot stop myself from thinking what else of hers I would like on my lips. I clear my throat and tear my gaze from her, jerking my head toward the pod closest to me. "Take this one."

All the Lokarian cadets follow her with their eyes as she walks briskly to the pod, running her small hands over the frame almost like a caress. I'm riveted by how she strokes the machine, and my cock hardens as I watch how lovingly she touches it.

Vlak. This is the champion hoverbike rider? She is nothing like I would have expected, and I clench my fists in frustration. Why couldn't she have been some butch woman with facial hair and a thick neck? Why did she have to be so…appealing?

When another male grunts in appreciation and the others laugh, I snap my head around, glowering at them. "You know the drills." I point to the pod track outside the open end of the dome. "Ten times around the track to warm up."

They reluctantly pull their attention from the new human female, snapping on earpieces that morph into protective bubbles of energy around their heads, mounting their pods, and accelerating out of the garage with only a few grunts and backward glances. I pivot on my heel and walk to Brooke, who's swung herself effortlessly up onto her pod.

"Not you."

She snaps her head up, her eyes level with mine. "Why not?"

My pulse quickens as her pupils darken with obvious anger. "I cannot let you out on the track. Not yet. I do not know your abilities."

She leans forward and gives me a small smile. "My *abilities* will put everyone here to shame."

"Really?" I can't help smiling at her self-assuredness. It isn't like the male bravado I'm used to with the Lokarian males. She knows she's good, and her confidence sends a thrill through me. I want nothing more than to see this small female ride my pods.

"That's right." She raises an eyebrow at me. "Unless you're afraid to let a woman show up your precious Lokarian cadets."

I want to tell her that they aren't *my* precious Lokarians, but watching her eyes flash makes my mouth go dry. If she's right and she does wipe the floor with the other cadets, I know exactly what they will do to her. Brooke Butler's life at the academy will be a living hell. Even if she's the best pod rider in the entire *vlakking* school, I can't let that happen to her.

I can't explain why I have an urge to protect her. Maybe it's because she's so small. Maybe it's because looking at her does something to me. Maybe it's because I know what it's like to be on the outside.

I grab her by the hips to lift her off the machine, my large hands spanning her waist and tingling from the contact. "Not today, human."

CHAPTER FIVE

Brooke

"What the hell?" I slap his hands as he attempts to pull me off the pod.

He stops tugging at me, his dark eyes meeting mine. Something flashes behind them for a moment before they harden. "I'm the instructor and you're the student, no matter how good you might think you are. And I say you're not riding today."

He's so close to me, the heat from his body pulses into me. I do my best not to notice just how spectacular a body it is, too. Unlike the other academy instructors I've had today, this guy isn't wearing a military uniform, and his bare arms are roped with muscle and etched with gold tattoos. Thick gold lines crawl up from under the neckline of his black T-shirt—a T-shirt that seems sculpted to the curves of his chest muscles and clings to his flat stomach. His hair is nearly black and falls around his neck, matching the scruff on his square jaw. This alien would look at home at any biker bar in Texas.

At the moment, I don't give a rat's ass how hot he is, or how him holding me by the waist makes my breath come out fast and shallow. All I care about is him letting go and letting me show him what I can do. I did not fly across the galaxy to watch a bunch of boys play. Sitting back and watching has never been my game.

"Get your hands off me," I growl. This isn't the first guy who'd pawed at me, and I have no problem showing him how Texas girls handle being groped.

He stills and lets go, holding up his hands and stepping back, but taking a long stride to position himself in front of the vehicle's nose. "Get off the pod."

Well, shit. Even if I start the pod, I can't go anywhere unless I want to plow him down. I don't think killing an instructor on my first day would work out well for me.

The Lokarians are still racing around the track, the sound of the pods a low hum in the distance as they flash white each time they pass the wide opening of the garage. Tears pricking the backs of my eyes as I watch them do what I love to do, and the unfairness of it makes me want to hit something. Preferably a dark-haired, bearded something.

I bite the inside of my mouth and will myself not to cry. No way is this asshole going to get tears from me. I can sense his gaze on me, and I jut my chin out as I swing myself off the pod and land on the ground, not deigning to look at him.

He exhales loudly. "Hoverbikes are not the same as Lokarian pods."

"Thanks for that news flash," I mumble under my breath, still refusing to glance at him.

He grunts and starts walking away from me, then pauses. "Well, are you coming?"

I debate whether or not to follow him, but what else do I have to do? As much as I want to storm out and go right to the head of the academy and complain, I'm not sure how things work around here, and if they'll even listen to me. I do know that this guy is the only pod instructor in the place, so if I piss him off too much, I'm screwed.

I follow him to a pod that's secured to the ground, and almost groan out loud. I must make some kind of discernable noise, because he twists around and looks at me.

"You're kidding, right?" I ask, after he stops in front of the training pod.

Crossing his arms over his chest, he angles his head at me. "Do you mean joking? Why would I make a joke about this?"

I wave at the machine. "This is something you use for someone who's never ridden a bike. I've been riding since I was eight years old."

"Not on these, you haven't."

I don't try to stop myself from rolling my eyes at this. "Your pods may be faster and more powerful, but they're nothing I can't handle." I cross my own arms over my chest, aware that I'm pushing my breasts up in the process and making them look pretty damn good. "Trust me, buddy, I'm used to riding things that are big and powerful."

His eyes darken dangerously, and I gulp. Shit. That was too far. What the fuck was I thinking? I sound like one of my brothers, and that is not a good thing.

He's a teacher, Brooke, I tell myself. And you, Miss Braggy, are a virgin who has *only* ever had hoverbikes between your legs.

Neither of us speak for a few moments, then he turns to the pod as if nothing has happened. "Unlike your hoverbikes, our pods have twin engines and can shift propulsion from one side to the other, all controlled by the grips on the handles." He reached up and touches the handle grips. "The steering is also more sensitive, which is why sudden movements aren't suggested. You want to ride these with your hips, not your shoulders."

I listen to his husky voice, but I can barely concentrate on his words. When he stops for a breath, I ask, "So, are you being a dick to me because I'm a human, or because I'm a female?"

He pivots slowly, and I have to suppress the urge to back up because the guy towers over me. "You think me doing my job as an instructor is me being a," he hesitates over the word, "dick to you?"

I don't back down. "Tell me honestly. Would you be doing this if one of the male cadets was a champion hoverbike racer? Or would you give him a chance to show you what he could do?"

He looms over me. "If I was afraid he might break his neck on a bike three times his size, I would make sure he knows what he's doing, first."

I don't believe him. And I know for a fact he wouldn't have grabbed a guy by his waist and tried to drag him off a pod. I'd hoped that the Lokarians would be more open-minded, since they're so much more technologically advanced than humans, but it's clear I was dead wrong about that.

For some reason I can't explain, I need to show this instructor that I know what I'm doing. I can't let him treat me like I'm not as good as I know I am. I've worked too hard to be kicked back to the starting line.

When he turns back to the pod and starts in on how the braking system works, I pick up an earpiece of a nearby rack. I hook it over my ear and press a button like I saw the other cadets do, pleasantly surprised when it becomes a bubble of energy that cocoons my head. Taking a few quick steps to an unused pod, I hop on. I flip the ignition and the pod roars to life between my thighs, sending a thrill through me.

The instructor whips around, his expression shocked, but before he can cross to me and try to pull me down again, I gun it, disengaging the magnetic clamps and shooting forward. He was right about them being powerful—and fast.

Within seconds, I'm zipping out of the garage and onto the track.

Even though I'm wearing one of their versions of a helmet, it's like there is nothing between my head and the air. I can't hear anything but the deafening rumble of my motor and the torrent of wind in my ears. I never ride without a helmet anymore, but the rush of the air in my face is one I remember from childhood, and suddenly I'm racing my brothers on the hot dirt track behind our house.

I fly past a pair of Lokarians, using my hips like the instructor said and cutting in front of them, then accelerating and leaving them both in the proverbial dust. It doesn't take long for me to get a feel for the machine and soon I'm lapping all the riders, bending low and using my small size to reduce air friction. My heart pounds and the growl of the engine vibrates my entire body, making my teeth rattle.

When I see that I'm the only one on the track, I slow my pod and exit, flying it evenly into the garage and parking it exactly where it had been. I'm heaving in breaths and trying to steady my breath when I realize that there is no other sound in the expensive space.

I glance up and my hammering heart stops. Every Lokarian is glaring at me, including the instructor. His eyes are practically sparking as he takes sharp steps toward me, and his hands are balled into hard fists.

So much for him being impressed by my ride. It looks like he couldn't give two shits that I blew by every other rider on the track my first time on a Lokarian pod. I press a button near my ear to disengage the energy helmet.

Unclenching one fist, he levels a finger at me. "You just earned yourself pod cleaning duty for the next week."

I open my mouth to protest, but his murderous expression makes me reconsider.

"Starting tonight at 1900 hours." He turns his back on me

and storms away as the Lokarian cadets snigger at me, their disapproval morphing into pleasure that I got called out and humiliated in front of the entire class. If I wasn't crazy about the instructor before, I really despise him now.

"Don't be even think of being late, human," he calls out over his shoulder.

CHAPTER SIX

Brooke

"I hate him," I whisper to Autumn, when I meet up with her in our next class.

"Your teacher?"

I nod as subtly as I can, trying not to draw the attention of the instructor. We're in our hand-to-hand combat class, which is held in another open space under a clear, domed ceiling. Black mats cover the floor—a contrast with the gleaming-white walls—but there isn't the scent of sweat I usually associate with a gym.

Flashing back to the pod instructor's furious expression when he'd ordered me to report to the garage to clean pods, I frown. "He's got it in for me."

Autumn shoots me a surprised look. "It's the first day. How can a teacher already have it in for you?"

I know I should admit to hijacking a pod and showing off, but I wouldn't have been forced to do that if the prick had treated me like the rest of the class. He wasn't going to give me a fair shake, even if I had stood there and listened to his boring lecture about pods. At least this way, he knows he was wrong about me. Which is probably why he was so pissed. An alpha guy like that does not like to be shown up by a woman.

I shrug. "I even got detention for a week."

Her mouth dangles open. "I didn't know they did that here."

"I wouldn't be surprised if they don't, and the pod instructor did it without authorization. He doesn't look like he follows the rules."

"I hear you on that. He definitely has a bad-boy vibe to him. Did you notice he doesn't wear the military uniform the rest of the teachers do?"

I've forgotten that my suite mates had their pod classes earlier than me—while I was being evaluated on the firing range—so she knows exactly what I'm talking about. I don't tell her that I noticed a whole lot about what the teacher was wearing—and how good he looked in it. I'm not admitting that to anyone.

Autumn runs a hand through her brown hair. "I'm glad I'm in the beginner class. All we did was practice getting on, and I wasn't so good at that."

"I'll coach you if you need help. So long as you don't mind hacking into the academy computer system and getting the pod instructor transferred to some remote moon."

She giggles and clamps a hand over her mouth as a few male cadets glance our way, then whispers out of one side of her mouth. "Consider it done."

I stare down a few of the guys who've glanced over at us, and they look away. The class seems to be made up entirely of human cadets, and I recognize the asshole from the shuttle who'd called me Red. At least he doesn't notice me and say anything.

This is the first class I've had with one of my suite mates, and I'm actually happy to see Autumn and catch up. She doesn't seem to be as excited, though.

"You okay?" I ask, as the tall Lokarian instructor steps onto the mat in his bare feet.

She bobbles her head—not a yes and not a no. "Hand-to-hand combat isn't exactly my thing."

"I'm sure it will be fine. All we have to do is be proficient enough to pass, right? They don't expect us to excel at everything. We're here because we're specialists."

"I guess." She doesn't sound convinced. "What if I don't pass?"

I'm about to tell her that of course she'll pass when the tall Lokarian with long, dark hair brushing the shoulders of his military uniform lets his gaze linger on us. We both throw our shoulders back as the instructor passes his eyes over us and then scans the rest of the class.

"This is hand-to-hand combat." His deep voice echoes off the curved glass ceiling. "This is not a lecture class. You will be expected to fight. You will sweat. Some of you will get injured. None of you will complain. Are there any questions?"

Autumn does not move, but I swear her breathing quickens.

The instructor unfastens his dark jacket and tosses it off to one side, revealing a tight, black T-shirt underneath that stretches across broad muscles and shows off impressive bronze arms. Unlike the thick, gold markings of the pod instructor, this Lokarian wears metallic bands around his wrists that wind up his forearms. It's hard not to stare, and I think it may just be the sexiest jewelry I've ever seen on a guy.

"I am Lieutenant Mikaeus of the Lokarian Fleet, and for the next term, I will be teaching you how to defend yourself and effectively attack in a hand-to-hand battle." He strides across the mat, his long legs eating up the floor. "I must warn you that Lokarian techniques are different from human ones. So, even if you think you are skilled in combat, I assure you there will be much you can learn."

He spins and beckons to the cadet who'd leered at me on the shuttle. "You."

The human with the buzz cut and the cocky grin steps forward. "McCabe, sir."

"McCabe." The Lieutenant starts to circle him, and the cadet's smile fades.

Lowering himself into a battle stance, McCabe mirrors the Lokarian, moving in the opposite direction.

"Humans telegraph their movements before they attack." The instructor's voice is low and even, as his eyes stay trained on the cadet. "A skilled opponent will see this and predict the blows, especially one with quicker reflexes. Like me."

I don't see the attack until the instructor has leapt into the air and hooked the cadet around the neck, bringing him down to the mat in a single, fast movement. McCabe's back slaps the mat hard, while the Lokarian lands gracefully on his feet. I'm reminded of a panther when he looks up at us and his lips curl in satisfaction as he hovers over the downed man.

We all suck in a breath and step back. Shit. Maybe Autumn's right. This doesn't look anything like grappling with my big brothers, even though they pinned me down enough times when I was growing up.

I eye the huge alien as he hoists McCabe to his feet. The cadet's face is red, and he looks both shocked and humiliated. I almost feel bad for the cocky bastard. Almost.

"I will teach you how to strike so that your opponent is taken by surprise." The Lokarian thumps McCabe on the back and sends him back to the group. "For now, pair off and let's see what you've got."

Autumn reaches for my hand before I can even turn to her. She has nothing to fear. We are the only women in the class, and no way am I fighting one of the guys from Earth who will want to prove himself to the Lokarian.

As the pairs move out across the mats, I lead Autumn to the corner. Hopefully, the badass instructor won't notice us as much off to the side, although I get the sense the intense alien doesn't miss much.

"Did you see that?" Autumn's voice cracks as she cuts her eyes to the Lokarian.

"Uh, yeah. It was hard to miss." I stretch my arms over my head to buy some time, as the other grappling partners around us begin to lunge at each other. "I don't think he expects us to be able to do *that*."

"I am so fluffed."

I give my head a small shake. "Do you mean fucked?"

Her cheeks color. "That too."

"I wouldn't worry about your lack of hand-to-hand combat skills, girl. Your lack of swearing skills is a much more immediate problem."

She tries to frown at me, but ends up smiling. The smile quickly drops, and I see what she sees—a flash of metallic arm bands as the instructor moves closer to us.

"Attack me," I tell her, extending one hand and flicking my fingers toward me.

"Seriously?"

"Unless you want me to make a run at you?"

She shakes her head. "No, you're small, but you look scrappy."

"I'm going to take that as a compliment, since I'm barely five feet." I urge her forward again. "Now come at me."

Autumn takes a deep breath and runs at me, diving for my middle and taking me down. I let her bring me to the mat before rearing up with my legs and flipping her onto her back. She emits a small shriek, as I pin her arms over her head.

A pair of legs appears in my peripheral vision, and we both

twist our heads to look over. Lieutenant Mikaeus is standing right next to us.

When I crane my neck to look up, he has his arms crossed over his chest and is scowling.

"Names?" he asks.

Autumn and I scramble to our feet and stand at attention.

"Butler," I say. "Brooke Butler."

His gaze slides to my friend, whose cheeks flush a deep scarlet.

"Autumn, I mean, Spencer. Cadet Spencer."

He doesn't utter another word, but turns around and walks away from us.

Autumn releases a breath. "What the holy hand grenade was that about?"

I don't know for sure, but I have the feeling neither of us are doing too well with the Lokarians so far.

CHAPTER SEVEN

Koran

I stomp into the instructor's dining room, unaware how fast and furiously I'm walking until heads swivel when I barrel inside.

Cool it, I tell myself, forcing a deep breath and slowing my pace.

But what was the female thinking? She could have broken her neck.

I flash back to the image of Brooke flying around the track, her body perfectly streamlined with the pod and her slightest movements steering it with precision. My pulse races, partly from anger that she openly defied me, and partly from arousal at how beautiful she looked when she came off the track, her hair wild and her eyes shining.

I curse at my body's weakness. I cannot be attracted to a student, no matter how appealing she might be. Especially one who clearly doesn't know how to listen, although if I'm being honest, that's part of what draws me to her.

I take a steadying breath and focus on the staff dining room, eager for a drink to take the edge off my frustration. Like a lot of spaces at the academy, this one is bright and white, with a domed ceiling. It perches on top of a tall spire and is reached by a fast elevator, giving it a bird's eye view of the rest of the campus and me a sudden sense of vertigo. One more reason I like pods instead of spaceships—closer to the ground.

I pause and scan the long, communal tables with serving robots zipping between them, carrying trays of steaming food. It's not that I'm uncomfortable eating with others. My clan always ate together. But this is not my clan, and I have yet to have a meal here that is not punctuated by awkward pauses and curious glances. I wish the dining room had a bar where I could sit and drink without drawing attention, but there are only long tables flanked with benches.

"Koran."

I turn toward the voice, expecting it to be Daryx, the head of the academy. It is not.

I walk toward the instructor I recognize as a member of the Kurvak clan. Unless I'm mistaken, he's the hand-to-hand combat instructor, although I don't recall his name. He wears the black Lokarian military uniform with its distinctive gold crest, but the jacket falls open at his throat, making me hope he might not be as stiff as the rest of my colleagues.

He nods to the seat across from him, and I sit.

"Mikaeus," he says by way of introduction.

"You were right about me. I'm Koran."

His gaze doesn't leave my face, and I remind myself that clan Kurvak has no issues with confidence, although I don't sense arrogance from him.

"You're the pod rider. I've heard about you."

I can't help bristling. "What have you heard?"

His eyebrow twitches almost imperceptibly. "That you're fast. The fastest Daryx has ever seen."

So, the head of the academy has been talking about me with this Lokarian? I wonder if they are friends or if the headmaster told everyone about me. I shrug as Mikaeus beckons a robot server. "I can hold my own."

"A modest Vratvos?"

Is he trying to provoke me? "Perhaps as rare as a humble Kurvak."

He stills, staring at me, then his face breaks into a wide smile, and he barks out a laugh. "Daryx said I would like you."

I don't know what to make of the fact that the Lokarians discussed me, and I shift on the hard bench as he orders Lokarian ales for us.

"How are you adjusting?" he asks, when the robot glides away. "I'm sure the academy is a big change."

He's right about that, but I don't want to admit how out of place I feel or how strange I find the rigid schedule and modern buildings. "It's an honor to be here."

From the quirk of his lips I can tell he knows I'm evading the question, but he doesn't press me. The ales arrive, and he takes a swig of his before leaning closer. "So, what do you think of these human cadets?"

Now that's an easy one. "They have much to learn. Out of all my classes today, only a handful have what it takes to be decent pod riders."

Mikaeus nods. "Agreed. Sometimes I wonder about this treaty. These humans are so much smaller and less developed than we are." His expression darkens. "And the females…"

I take a long draw from my ale, welcoming the cool tang of the drink and then emitting a low grunt before I can stop myself. "Are unlike Lokarian females."

"How could the Earthlings think these tiny creatures could be anything but a hinderance?"

I think back to Brooke Butler flying around the pod track like nothing I had ever seen before and I take another swallow of ale. "They are not unskilled, but they are not warriors, either."

The Kurvak leans back, shaking his head. "You should have seen a few of them attempting to grapple today. I do not know how they will pass my class."

"Maybe this experiment will not continue. If the humans cannot meet our standards, we cannot risk the strength of our fleet. Not against the Skrum."

The combat instructor scrapes a hand through his long hair. "We cannot fail. We need to train these humans so they can lead their own troops against the enemy. Their weakness means our collective demise."

I blow out a long breath, hating what he says but knowing he is right. The Skrum need Earth. If they harvest its water, it will fuel and strengthen their swarm. It is crucial we stop them, which means we must train the humans in our advanced skills and technology. No matter how frustrating it is to us.

"Some of them have guts," I admit. "One of the female cadets in my advanced class hijacked a pod and raced the track."

His mouth falls open. "I heard some of the Lokarian cadets talking about this. What is a human female doing in your advanced class?"

"She is a champion hoverbike racer on Earth."

Mikaeus's eyes widen. "And? Can she ride pods as well as she rides their hoverbikes?"

I cannot lie. "I have rarely seen anyone ride as well, including Lokarians."

"Is she better than you, Koran?"

I straighten at this, frowning. "Doubtful."

He grins and drains the rest of his ale. "Well, I hope you punished her for her disobedience. A champion or not, cadets cannot get away with challenging us."

"She will be cleaning pods for the rest of the week."

He gives me an approving nod.

I do not tell him that the slight female has been the only thing I can think about, and that the image of her slim legs wrapped around the pod makes my cock swell. Being attracted to one of the humans would not help how the other Lokarian instructors view me. Admitting that I find the tiny creature appealing would only prove to them how I don't fit in.

I look around and see that the other instructors are no longer giving me sidelong glances. It seems that the approval of this Kurvak instructor has made me one of them. At least for now. I do not want to do anything to damage this.

Taking another swallow of my ale, I wonder what my Vratvos brothers would think if they could see me. Would they be shocked that an elite Kurvak with gold bracelets winding up his arms is sitting with me and that we are talking as equals? It is not what we expect from Kurvaks, or other clans. We are used to distrust and scorn, but I sense none from Mikaeus. For a brief moment, I wonder if I have been the one in the wrong. Have I been holding the other Lokarians at arm's length because of my own prejudice?

He stands. "I should return to the mats." Eyeing my exposed arms, he thumps me on the bicep. "If you ever want a sparring partner, I'd be honored to enter the ring with you."

For a Lokarian, sparring with another indicates trust and brotherhood. I'm startled by his offer and give him a sharp bow of my head. "The honor would be mine."

He returns my bow, then turns and leaves the dining room. I remain for a moment, stunned by the Kurvak's actions. Warmth fills my chest, as I'm struck by something I haven't experienced since I left my clan to come to the academy. Belonging.

I give a final look out the clear dome of the space and down onto the buildings of the campus, spotting my garage and pod track on the outer edge. Maybe this job isn't so bad, after all.

I stride out of the dining room and step onto the high-speed elevator. My stomach lurches slightly when it drops down, but I find that I'm getting used to the lightning-fast descent, and I no longer want to vomit once I reach the ground level.

Stepping out of the open doors, I nod at a pair of clan Droq instructors entering the compartment, their silver tattoos glinting. The sun is setting, and warm light casts an orange glow over the campus, the mirrored tiles of the buildings reflecting the color and the clear domes glistening.

I take long steps toward my pod track, but I am no longer fuming about the human. A buzzing from the device in my pocket jolts me out of my good mood, and I reluctantly pull it out and glance down at the Lokarian symbols flashing across the small, flat screen.

I sigh. I have no choice but to answer it, even though I want nothing more than to ignore it. Peering around me to make sure I am out of earshot of any other Lokarians, I accept the transmission.

"Koran?" The voice is guttural and rough.

"Yes, Glatzor," I reply, making sure to sound respectful to the leader of clan Vratvos, even as I dread what I know he will ask.

"So," he growls. "How is our plan coming along? Have you done what we have asked?"

CHAPTER EIGHT

Brooke

I report to the garage right on time—after double-checking that 1900 means the same in Lokarian military time as it does on Earth, even though days on Lokar are only twenty-two hours, and their hours aren't as long as ours—but the cavernous space is dimly lit and echoes my footsteps. A shiver dances up my spine. The only thing keeping me from bolting is the familiar scent of fuel and metal that makes me think of my father's garage.

I push a pang of homesickness out of my mind as I walk past an anchored pod, running my fingers over the cool surface. I can't afford to give in to the loneliness of being so far away from everything I know and everyone I love. I'm here to train so I can hopefully help save my planet. There's no room for a pity party, even if my first day was a disaster. I'm not here to be liked or be the teacher's pet, I remind myself, which is good because so far the Lokarian instructors don't seem too crazy about me.

I peer around the darkened domain of the pod instructor. Especially this asshat.

I felt a little better about my day after confiding in Autumn and a lot better about meeting up with all of my suite mates at dinner. Over a strangely spicy Lokarian stew, we'd exchanged horror stories about our first day at the academy. The only one of us who hadn't struggled with any of her classes had been Elena, but the mysterious woman with the long, dark braid seemed skilled at keeping a low profile.

My new friends hadn't been shocked when I'd told them about taking the pod to show what I could do, although Layla had told me I should be glad I only got pod cleaning duty. She'd also told me that I was a fucking badass bitch—causing Autumn to blush—so I took that as a compliment. Even though I'm not used to having female friends, the women are definitely growing on me. I think of them back in our suite, hanging out and laughing some more about the day, and I wish I was with them.

I squint into the darkness and hear nothing. Drawing in a deep breath, I turn on my heel. "Fuck this asshole."

"Hello to you, too." The huge Lokarian with the gold tattoos is standing right behind me, and I almost walk into him.

I put up my hands to brace myself on his chest and stumble. He grabs me by the wrists to steady me, but holds tight even when I've righted myself.

His touch pulses into me, making me almost shiver again. I jerk my hands. "Let go of me."

He releases me with a slight tilt of his head. "Just trying to keep you from injuring yourself, human."

I step back, my cheeks hot. "You don't need to worry about me getting hurt. I'm tougher than I look."

He studies me, his eyes glittering in the shadows of the room. "We'll see."

I huff out a breath and glare at his back as he turns and walks away. Like in class, he stops after a few steps, twists around, and looks at me. "Are you coming?"

Muttering a few choice words, I hurry to catch up as he takes off again. Shit, he has long legs. My gaze drifts up from his legs to his ass. And a really nice ass.

When he reaches the end of the row of pods, he reaches down and grabs a towel out of a steel bin, tossing it to me with barely a glance in my direction. Then he turns and tosses a round, flat canister at me.

I snatch it from the air, glad for my quick reflexes. "What's this?"

"Pod wax." He sweeps an arm at the long row of machines. "They all need a coat."

My shoulders sag. Waxing all these is going to take hours. I clench my teeth as I catch him watching me. He's probably waiting for me to whine so he can tell everyone that the human female couldn't cut it. Well, no way am I giving him that satisfaction.

"Great." I twist off the metal lid then eye him. "You want to move out of my way so I can get to work?"

He steps aside, and I ignore the quiver on one side of his mouth.

If this Lokarian thinks he can break me by not letting me ride and by making me polish his bikes until my arms are numb, he's in for a big surprise. I dip the cloth in the iridescent, silver polish and start rubbing it onto the body of the first pod in circular motions.

The wax isn't like wax on Earth. It almost melts into the metal, making the hard surface glimmer for a moment before it vanishes. I stare, fascinated, then swirl some more wax onto the pod.

"Is this how you wax hoverbikes on your Earth?" His voice is so close to my ear I almost jump. How is someone so big able to sneak up on me like he does?

I swivel my head, and he's hovering over me. I would move away from him, but there's nowhere to go but onto the bike.

"Yes." My ire flares. "You have a problem with it?"

"Lokarian wax needs to be applied in long strokes."

I glare at him. I know he's making this shit up just so he can find one more thing to criticize me for.

He lets out his own impatient breath, reaching for my hand and taking it in his. I give a small yelp, but he's too strong for me to pull away. He guides my hand with the cloth into the wax canister then lifts it to the surface of the pod. Pressing both our hands onto the metal, he moves the cloth down the shiny, white body. The shimmering wax seeps into the surface and the curved side of the pod almost glows.

My heart hammers in my chest as he leans so close to me his body almost cocoons mine. I've never had a guy this big be so close, and I know it would take almost no effort on his part to overpower me. This is usually the point where one of my brothers would step in and fists would fly. Actually, it never gets to this point back home. Any guy within fifty miles learned to steer clear of me a long time ago. But this isn't Texas, and my brothers are light years away.

I remember how easily he'd grabbed my waist in class. Lokarians clearly don't have the same concept of personal space as humans. He's not hitting on you, I tell myself. He's just a dick who's trying to intimidate you. Still, I hope he can't feel my pulse racing or my hand trembling.

"See?" He points to the area I'd waxed in circles that looks dull by comparison.

I wish I could think of a smart comeback, but my mouth has gone dry. I nod, shaking his hand off mine and clearing my throat. "Got it."

He steps back, but I refuse to look at him, as I even out my breathing and focus on the pod. I hate that my palms are sweaty and my hand buzzes from where he touched it. I should *not* have this reaction to an instructor. Especially one who's such a bossy asshole.

I dip the cloth into the wax and draw it down the length of the pod, repeating the action until one side is polished to a shine. I straighten and smile at my work, my back aching.

"Not bad," he says from behind me. "Only twenty more to go."

I shoot him a murderous look, but walk quickly around to the other side of the pod and get to work. "Is your plan to have me do this every night?"

"I do not need them waxed every night."

I glance up at where he's standing on the other side of the pod with his arms crossed, gold ink covering most of his biceps. Hope flutters in my chest. Maybe this guy isn't such a jerk after all. "So, I don't have to come back tomorrow night?"

"Oh, you will come back tomorrow night. That is when your class is."

"Wait, what?" The cloth slips out of my hand. "What about the advanced class I was in today?"

"You are no longer in that class."

This is a punch to my gut. "You're kicking me out of the advanced class? All because I rode your stupid pod without permission?"

"That is not why." He levels his gaze at me, and his eyes flash dark. "But it is for your own good."

I want to kick the patronizing prick in the balls for thinking he knows what's good for me. And who says I want to spend my evenings doing more work with this jerk? I may be here to learn how to race pods, but this is ridiculous. I did not sign up for this, and I'm about to tell him so when he spins around and strides away. I mutter a few choice words under my breath as I watch.

"If you are going to call me something, human," he calls back over his shoulder. "I prefer Koran to asshole."

Well too fucking bad, asshole.

CHAPTER NINE

Brooke

"Can he do that?" Layla asks, flipping her long, black hair over her shoulder as we walk across campus the next morning.

"I have no idea. I guess he just did." I lower a pair of sunglasses over my eyes as the sun crests the jagged peaks of the obsidian mountain range in front of us. The Lokarian sun isn't as bright as ours on Earth, but it's still morning, and I am definitely not a morning person. As soon as the rays of light hit the mirrored tiles of the building and refract off the clear domes that seem to dot the entire campus, it will be blinding.

Autumn shakes her head, her face creased with worry. "You should talk to someone. I wouldn't want to have to take classes alone with that guy."

I lift my cup of hot Lokarian tea to my lips, wishing it was coffee, but not willing to drink the half-ass, alien substitute. "I'm not scared of him." That's not entirely true, but I'm more scared of my own reaction to him than anything. "But why should I have to take classes at night?"

"You want me to do something about it?" Elena asks, her gray eyes intense as she takes a swig from her own cup. Elena drinks the thick Lokarian version of java, which means she's definitely tougher than me—or doesn't have taste buds.

I'm not sure what exactly she means about "doing something about it" but I have a feeling it's not talking. I still don't have a good handle on Elena's specialty, but I suspect it's something pretty deadly, and I get the sense she's excellent at it.

I wave a hand all my friends as we walk four across down the paved path toward the main building. "No. I don't want to make it worse."

"What would be worse than night classes?" Autumn asks.

I gulp down the last of my tea and the hot, spicy liquid burns my throat. "Getting kicked out or not allowed to ride pods at all. At least this way, the dickwad is going to teach me."

"Come to think of it." Autumn glances over her shoulder and waits for a pair of hulking Lokarian cadets to pass us. "I'd rather take my hand-to-hand combat classes at night where no one else could see me."

I put an arm around her shoulders. "You aren't *that* bad."

She shoots me a side eye glance. "Come on, Brooke. I'm awful. If anyone's going to get kicked out for failing a class, it will be me."

Layla shakes her head, hard. "They can't kick you out. You're a fucking computer genius. We need more of you to figure things out."

Elena nods thoughtfully. "She's right. We aren't going to defeat the Skrum with impressive grappling. They're a swarm."

We're all quiet for a moment, no doubt thinking of the horrific aliens determined to attack Earth and literally suck her dry.

"So," I finally break the silence as we reach the imposing

metal arch that extends out over the main building like an awning. "What classes do you all have this morning?"

Our schedules rotate, so we don't have each class every day. I know I start off today with basic flight, and I'm looking forward to seeing what that means. I can't imagine that we'll be learning to fly Lokarian spaceships, but maybe we'll be given a basic understanding of the different types of ships they use. I know some of them put even our most sophisticated jets to shame.

Layla pauses once we've walked inside the high-ceilinged space, her gaze instinctively going to the towering dome and crisscrossing metal walkways. "Shooting, which is right in my fucking wheelhouse."

"Hand-to-hand." Elena grins, and I guess she doesn't have any fear of grappling. One look at her tall, athletic frame makes me think she can hold her own, even against a Lokarian.

"Good luck," Autumn mutters, before adding, "I've got explosives."

Layla exhales loudly. "Lucky bitch."

A Lokarian seems startled as he passes us—his eyebrows popping up—but Elena shoots him a look that makes him keep moving.

"You get the feeling these aliens aren't used to badass women?" Layla asks.

Autumn glances at the device hooked to her waist. "Shoot. We're going to be late." She backs away with a wave. "Catch you all at dinner."

I try to remember the fastest way to the flight-simulation classroom, as I watch my friends dart off in different directions. Falling in behind a human cadet with short, sandy-brown hair, I snake my way through the hallways leading off the main foyer.

We make a sharp turn down a hallway, and the guy twists around. "Are you following me?"

He doesn't look upset or aggressive. Actually, he looks amused.

"That depends," I say. "Are you headed to flight class?"

"Yep." He extends a hand. "Cadet Carter, tour guide, at your service."

I shake his hand, pleased to recognize a slight twang in his American accent. "Cadet Butler. Stalker extraordinaire."

He laughs and the corners of his eyes crinkle. He's cute, in a wholesome kind of way. "Then right this way, Cadet Butler. I think we're almost there."

At the end of a final, long hall that takes us to what must be the farthest end of the building, we reach the flight classroom. Carter waves his arm in an exaggerated, gallant sweep, and I walk through the double doors with him behind me.

When I'd been given the tour of the academy, the Lokarian guide had only waved at the classroom. We hadn't looked inside. Now I take a second to take in the theatre-style room that overlooks a giant hangar bay filled with ships of all kinds. Through the clear overlook, I see shuttles like the one we arrived on, sleek jets with pointed noses, and larger, gray-hulled vessels with curved wings that remind me of a bat.

Carter moves past me and slides into an available seat. I see that we're the last to arrive and the Lokarian instructor is already standing at the front of the room, his arms behind his back. Like all the aliens, he's big and brawny, but this one looks clean-cut, with short hair, and no noticeable tattoos or adornments. I slip into the seat next to Carter and ignore the glances coming our way.

Once I'm sitting, I realize that these aren't normal seats. There is an instrument panel in front of us, as well as controls in the wide-set arms. The backs are high, and a clear dome can flip over them to create a makeshift cockpit. A thrill goes through me at the thought of experiencing the Lokarian version of a flight simulator.

"Welcome to beginning flight. I'm Captain Kulvar." The instructor's voice easily carries up the rows of seats. "I'm here to teach you how to fly Lokarian space vessels." He turns and peers across the hangar bay. "There are those of you who will go on to pilot your own ships, but all of you must know the basics of operating every vessel."

Carter shifts next to me, and gives me a quick smile.

"If you have never flown with instruments before, this might be a challenge for you." The instructor's gaze rests on the humans in the class. "But I expect you all to reach proficiency by the end of the term."

I glance at the instrument panel. None of the symbols are familiar to me, but I hope the instincts I've honed working with hover bikes will come in handy. I rub my palms down the front of my pants.

"Ever flown before?" Carter whispers, his eyes going to me wiping off my sweaty palms.

I shake my head. "You?"

"Nope. I'm Navy, but not a pilot."

I'm about to tell him that he's not nearly as cocky as some of the Seals, who are also at the academy, but the instructor's voice booms again.

"The consoles in front of you should be activated. Place your thumb on the green pad so it can scan your biometrics."

I do what he says, but nothing happens. I glance over at Carter, but he's also holding his thumb down, with no apparent result.

"Are we doing something wrong?" I ask, my voice low. "Or do the scanners not read humans?"

We both look around, but the Lokarian cadets also seem frustrated, their faces pinched as they jam their thumbs on the pads repeatedly.

The instructor grumbles loudly, taking long steps over to a podium and tapping away at something. After a moment, he frowns. "Never mind that for now. I guess we're going to get you all into some ships."

My pulse trips. We're flying today?

"Come on." Carter tugs my sleeve as he stands.

I jump up and follow him and the rest of the class down the steps and then out into the hangar bay. Like the pod garage, it smells of fuel and steel, with the familiar sounds of clanging and scraping to match.

The Lokarian instructor strides in front of us, slapping his hand on the side of a fighter. "Our L-356. Warp-and-stealth capable." He points to a pair of Lokarians. "You two. In the cockpit."

As the two cadets scramble into it, the instructor continues to the next ship, placing a hand on the gunmetal-gray hull. "This may look unassuming, but this bomber can carry enough payload to bring down a battleship." He cuts his eyes to me and Carter. "You two. Ready to try it out?"

I hesitate, sure he was going to pair me off with the other female human I'd spotted in the class and assign us to some rickety, puddle-jumping shuttle.

"Problem, Cadet?" The Lokarian's gaze bores into me. "I have no intention of treating you humans any differently."

"No problem, sir." I'm so happy at his words I could cheer. All I want is to be treated the same as the rest of the cadets.

As I follow Carter up the ramp into the dark interior of the bomber, my heart is pounding. Not only have I found a Lokarian who's willing to teach me like everyone else, I have a new reason to hate the pod instructor who won't.

CHAPTER TEN

Koran

I lean against one of my pods in the dark, relieved that classes are over, and the garage is quiet. After a day filled with the sounds of pods accelerating out of the building and whizzing around the track, I'm grateful that there is no sound but my own deep breaths.

I heave in the cool, evening air and rub a hand across my forehead. Glatzor's call has rattled me more than I want to admit—even to myself—and I'm glad there was no one else around to hear it. I do not know what will happen if anyone at the academy discovers I am still in contact with the head of the Vratvos. It may not be a crime to talk with members of my clan, but it is well known that Glatzor works only for the benefit of clan Vratvos and has no love for Lokarian leadership—or its prized military academy.

If only they knew, I think, bracing my hands behind me on the hard metal of the pod and slumping my shoulders forward.

If they knew why I am really here they would send me packing —or worse.

Glatzor's words repeat in my mind. "You must find out what they're developing. They will not be able to hold their technological superiority over us if we know what they have."

Even if I wanted to betray the head of the academy who recruited me and the other Lokarians like Mikaeus who have befriended me, how would I do what my leader asks? I am a pod racer. I know nothing about the systems where this information would be kept. I don't even know *where* the systems or computers are kept.

I spin around and slam an open palm against the pod, the sharp sound echoing through the cavernous space and my hand stinging from the blow. "They expect too much from me."

Throat clearing from behind startles me and makes me freeze.

"Is this a bad time?" The female voice asks. "I thought you said 1900, and it's 1900—"

"I know what I said." I round on her, wanting to take my frustration out on something or someone. I've forgotten I told the human pod racer to come back at night. It seemed like the perfect solution at the time, but now, the last thing I want is to teach another human. All I want is to drown myself in a glass of Lokarian gin.

Her pupils widen, then she puts her hands on her hips and glares at me. "Why don't we forget about this stupid idea of night classes, and I'll go back to the advanced class, like I'm supposed to?"

I shake my head. I know what the Lokarian cadets think of her, and I know that an arrogant, male Lokarian can make her life miserable or put her in danger. Neither one I'm willing to risk. "No. It's better this way."

"For who? You?" She throws her arms open wide. "No

offense, but I don't want to spend my nights alone with you in a dark garage."

It's obvious from the look of distaste on her face that she does not like me. I know this should not bother me, but it does. I'm only trying to protect her, yet she clearly despises me for it. "You can drop out. Not every human will make it through the term."

Her eyes narrow and her cheeks flush. "You'd like that, wouldn't you?"

"Why do you think I would get pleasure out of that?"

She steps closer to me. "It's obvious you have it in for me. No other Lokarian teacher refuses to teach me with the rest of the class. I asked around. There isn't a single other cadet who has to take separate night classes because the instructor is afraid to be shown up by one of his students."

Anger flares in my chest. "You think I'm doing this because I'm threatened by you?"

She shrugs. "What else is it?" She holds up her fingers and starts counting off, her voice getting louder and louder. "You refused to let me show you I could ride, and when I did it anyway and outperformed all of your teacher's pets, you punished me for it. Everything I do around you is wrong, including how I wax a pod."

When she stops, she's practically screaming, and her chest is heaving. I fight the urge to let my gaze drift to the cleavage peeking out of the top of her scoop-neck T-shirt, and I focus instead on the hollow of her throat and the pulse I can see throbbing in her neck.

I'm not used to being yelled at, especially not by students, and even less so by human females. Her accusations that the Lokarian cadets are my teacher's pets is laughable but still enrages me. I am doing this to protect her from them. How dare she suggest I prefer those cocky males who look down on me as much as they look down on her?

"You do not know what you're talking about." I grit out the words, forcing myself to stay calm. If she was a male, I would have hit her already. The Vratvos solve most problems with fists, so I am unused to anger not being followed with a bloody fight. "I'm protecting you."

"I don't need protecting! I'm a grown woman, not some little helpless girl!"

Blood is pounding in my ears, but I don't know anymore if it's because I'm furious or aroused. I know very well that she's a grown woman, but she doesn't know what these cadets are like. She doesn't know what they've already said about her. As I watch her breath deeply, a flush crawling up the exposed skin of her chest, I can't help thinking how pretty she is when she wants to claw my eyes out.

She doesn't back down, taking another step to close the gap between us and tipping her head up slightly to hold my gaze. "I know I'm good at this." She flicks her eyes to the pods. "And I know I'm not going to let some big bully keep me from doing what I'm good at."

"You think I'm a bully? I thought I was an asshole."

"You're both," she spits out, her hands in fists by her side.

I straighten suddenly, and she almost stumbles back. "I'm also the only pod instructor at this academy." I walk forward as she backs up. "And a fucking amazing rider, myself." She bumps up against an anchored pod, but I don't stop walking until I'm towering over her. "I've seen what you can do, human." I lean down until my lips are next to her ears. "But you have no idea what I can do."

When I move my head back, her eyes are wide as she studies my face, finally locking on my lips and licking her own. Panic flutters in my stomach as I realize I'm playing with fire, and this human may be more impulsive than even I anticipated. I begin to step back, but she reaches one hand up and rakes it through my hair, jerking my mouth to hers before I can stop her.

This is wrong, I think, before the softness of her lips and the sweet taste of her obliterates any coherent thought in my brain. I part her lips with a quick sweep of my tongue, taking control of the kiss and wrapping both arms around her. Lifting her up onto the pod in a single motion, I pull her into me as she circles her legs around my waist.

My cock aches as I rock into her, but when she groans into my mouth, I stop. I tear my mouth from hers and look down at her dazed expression.

This is wrong.

I can't ignore it this time. She is a student—a human student—and I cannot fuck her on a pod. I cannot fuck her anywhere. My place at this academy—which is the only chance I've ever had at a real life—is precarious enough.

"You're right." Her voice is breathy as she smiles up at me. "I had no idea."

I shake my head as I lift her down off the pod and step away from her. "I'm sorry."

"Why are you apologizing? I'm the one who kissed you."

"I never should have responded the way…" I cross my hands in front of my cock as it strains against my pants. "I'm sorry. You should go."

She blinks up at me. "But what about class? I actually did come here to learn. Is that a no-go, too?"

"I'm sorry, Brooke." Saying her name is almost painful, as I force myself to turn and walk away from her.

CHAPTER ELEVEN

Brooke

"You need me to do what?" Autumn blinks at me.

I cast a furtive glance around the wide hallway as cadets pass us, their boots thumping the floor. "I just want a peek at the progress reports."

"By having me hack into the academy computers?"

I shrug. "I mean, yeah. I know you don't have your laptop on you, but we're so close to the computer lab. I swear, it will take two seconds. One tiny peek at one class and that's it."

She doesn't look convinced. "Is this about that teacher you can't stand? Is he still giving you a hard time?"

I can't admit what actually happened with Koran, but she's right that it's his class I want to check up on. I overheard a couple of instructors talk about logging in the cadets' progress from the first few days, and I need to be sure that I'm getting credit for my private pod classes, even though I technically haven't taken one.

"Of course, it is." I hold up a hand. "And before you tell me to ask him directly, that won't work." Because I'm not sure I won't try to kiss him again, is what I don't say out loud.

She lets out a sigh, but I can tell she's weakening. I put my hands together as if I'm in prayer and give her my best puppy dog eyes.

Autumn shakes her head, looking both disgusted and amused. "Does that ever actually work on people?"

"I don't know," I say. "You tell me."

She tugs me by the sleeve down the hall and toward the computer lab. "This is a one-time thing, right?"

"Absolutely."

We duck through a glass door and into the quiet room where only a few cadets sit working at long tables in front of holographic screens. No one bothers to look up when we enter, so Autumn pulls me to the back of the room.

She sits on one of the swivel stools, tapping a panel in the desk and activating both the holographic keyboard and the screen, which flickers in the air. I'm amazed by how quickly she works—and by the cool Lokarian tech. Within minutes, she's managed to access the academy systems, find a backdoor through the firewall, and is scrolling through class progress reports.

"What's the name of the class?" she whispers.

"Advanced pod. The afternoon section, if that matters."

"It doesn't."

Another minute and a roster pops up onto the floating screen. I stare at it, then turn to Autumn. "It's in Lokarian."

"Duh." She shakes her head at me before tapping more keys and the letters begin morphing into English. "I can only maintain the translation for a minute, so read fast."

I concentrate on the words as I scan the list from top to bottom. Each cadet's name has a series of numbers to the right, which I'm guessing is Koran's evaluation of their abilities. I see

Carter's name and a bunch of high 90s next to his name. I grin, happy that my friend is doing so well. It doesn't mean I still don't want to kick his ass on the pod track, but I'm glad to see he'll be able to hold his own.

I continue to search, but I soon realize I'm not even on there. Before I'm about to tell Autumn we must have the wrong class, I see a line at the bottom, separated from the rest.

Butler, Brooke

I'm not thrilled to be on a line separated from the rest of the class, but at least I'm there. My gaze slides to the right, and my heart stops.

Status TBD

"What the fuck does that mean?"

Autumn tries to follow my gaze. "What does what mean?"

I point to the line with my name. "That. It's total bullshit."

She frowns when she reads it. "Well, at least it's not a bad grade."

"I shouldn't get a bad grade or a status TBD or anything close to that in pod class." My voice rises, and a couple of people turn around. "It's the whole fucking reason I'm here!"

Autumn's fingers fly across the holographic keyboard, and the screen disappears. "So, what are you going to do now?"

All thoughts of kissing Koran have left my mind. I don't care about being embarrassed or apologizing or any of that. "I'm going to find that cocky son of a bitch and tell him exactly what he can do with his 'status TBD.'"

My friend lets out a weary breath. "Oh, crap on a cracker."

CHAPTER TWELVE

Koran

I stand under my shower, letting the nearly scalding water pound my shoulders. It's been a long day, and my muscles are tight from demonstrating fast pivots on the pods.

I lean my palms flat against the slick tile, the heat uncoiling my shoulders as I try to think about anything but what my mind has continued to return to, since the moment I sent her away. Brooke Butler and the taste of her sweet mouth have filled my thoughts all day.

"Vlak!" I slap my hand on the wall, welcoming the sharp sting. How did I let this happen? How could I let myself be so weak?

Vratvos are never weak, especially with females. We take what we want and never get attached. So why is this female—and a human female, at that—all I can think about?

I bow my head and let the water cascade down, my cock swelling at the thought of her small body against mine. I guess it doesn't matter now. I'm finally somewhere it's appropriate to have a rock-hard erection.

Reaching down, I grasp my cock, my hand sliding easily down the long shaft. My eyes are closed, and I can see her, her face tipped back to look at me, her plump lips slightly parted and her breathing shallow. My body quivers as I stroke hard.

I know the look of desire in a female's eyes. Brooke wanted me, and she wanted me to do more than kiss her.

I let out a strangled moan as my hand bumps across my ribbed flesh. I want to be burying it inside the human, not plea-suring myself, but I also know that to do that would be breaking just about every rule I vowed to uphold when I came to the academy.

As if you aren't already violating your vows, a voice hisses in the back of my head.

I force that voice away. Even though I know my clan wants me here for their own reasons, what they don't know—would never suspect—is that I am here for me. I have never had the chance to do something good and help my people by using my talents, and I can't throw that opportunity away. But I can put off the demands of the Vratos and decide never to touch her again.

Touching isn't the same as fantasizing, though, and I plan to imagine myself fucking Brooke in a thousand different ways. I squeeze my eyes tighter, as I picture her small, lithe body strad-dling a pod, the engine roaring between her legs. Watching her ride a pod had almost made me come on the spot in the garage, and remembering her joy-ride has my cock jerking. I let out a bellow as my release overtakes me, blinding me with its sudden fury. When I finally open my eyes and uncoil my hand from my cock, there is a faint pounding noise coming from outside the bathroom.

Cursing, I flip off the water and step out of the shower. The only person who could be visiting my instructor quarters is

Mikaeus, who suggested we grab a drink. I pull a dark towel from a nearby rack, hooking it loosely around my waist and not bothering to dry off as I leave the bathroom.

"Come," I call out, knowing Mikaeus will not care if I am not properly attired.

I cross in front of the bed to the ebony dresser that stretches underneath the window overlooking the obsidian mountains. The door slides open as I'm digging in a drawer.

"Who the fuck do you think you...?" Brooke is halfway across my room when I turn to face her.

Her gaze drops to my bare chest and low-slung towel. She clamps her mouth shut, and her face reddens.

I'm only glad my cock isn't tenting the towel, as I appraise the female standing in my room in her snug, dark pants and tank top. "I think I'm the only one who belongs in this room. What are you doing here?"

The door swishes shut behind her, and she takes a step back, clearing her throat. "I couldn't find you down in the garage, so I asked where the instructor quarters are. Then a guy pointed out your room to me."

"So, half the campus knows you were coming to my private quarters?"

Her eyes flash. "It's not like that."

I cross to her, the heat in her gaze making my pulse quicken. "You didn't come for more?"

Brooke takes another step back. "You wish."

I cannot stop myself from touching her. Or for loving how beautiful she is when she's angry. I trace a finger down one of her soft cheeks. "You're right. I do wish."

Her pupils flicker. "Well, tough luck. I'm here to talk about the fact that you haven't updated my progress report."

That stops me. "What?"

"You heard me. I know you've given everyone else grades. But not me. So, what gives?"

I do not know how she knows this, but she's right. I eye this human with her jaw set and her fists clenched. I am not used to be challenged, and definitely not by a female. Despite knowing I cannot have her, I want her even more.

"Aside from the stunt you pulled the first day, I have not seen you ride," I say.

"And whose fucking fault is that?"

"Mine." I take a step closer until my body is almost brushing hers. "I promise you there is nothing I want more than to see you ride."

She swallows, her gaze never leaving mine. "I don't like cocky guys."

"No?" I don't touch her, but she leans in closer to me.

She shakes her head. "Just because I kissed you that once doesn't mean I want to…"

"Want to…?" I tilt my head and lower my voice. "Want to what, Brooke? Fuck me?"

Brooke inhales sharply then lifts her hands to press them against my still-damp chest. "That kiss was a mistake. I never should have done it."

I drop my head so that it's next to hers. "I don't know about that. I liked it, and I'm pretty sure you did, too."

"This is such a fucking mistake," she murmurs, as she turns her face and wraps her arms around my neck, pulling my mouth to hers.

Her movement is so quick, it takes me a moment to respond, but I encircle her with my arms and lift her off the floor. I part her lips with my tongue and deepen the kiss, the taste of her making my cock harden almost instantly. She moans into me, and I grind my body against hers, the towel coming loose and slipping off my waist.

After a few moments, she pulls away, looking up at me with wide eyes. She then looks down to where the only thing keeping the towel from hitting the floor is the hard bar of my cock. "Holy fuck!"

My breath is uneven, but my head is already starting to clear. "Brooke."

She waves her hands as she backs away. "It was a mistake to come here. This was all another big mistake."

She turns, opening the door and running out of my quarters before I can stop her.

I pull the towel off my cock and throw it to the floor. I don't know what is wrong with me, but I need to get a grip on this student and why I can't seem to control myself around her. I cannot afford to lose my focus. Or my heart.

"Vlakking hell." I scrape a hand through my wet hair. "This female is going to ruin me."

CHAPTER THIRTEEN

Brooke

"Earth to Butler. Or should I say, Lokar to Butler?"

I lift my head and see Carter eyeing me. We're back in the cockpit of the bomber we've been assigned to in flight class, doing a diagnostic scan of the systems before we fire her up. "Sorry. Were you asking me something?"

He laughs. "Yeah, but don't sweat it. The ship hasn't blown up yet."

I sag in my seat. "Shit. That bad?"

It's been a day since I ran out of Koran's room, and I can't stop thinking about him, or how fucking stupid I was to kiss him. Again. My face burns as I think about the look on his face when I backed away from him. He'd looked like he'd just made the biggest mistake of his life. It was the same look he'd had when he'd walked away from me in the garage. So, why does he keep kissing me, I wondered? Or kissing me back, I guess.

I'm also still confused by the fact that I thought I saw Layla—

or at least a flash of hair that looked like hers—going into one of the instructor's rooms as I was leaving Koran's quarters, but I can't imagine why she would be there. I must have been seeing things in my flustered state because Layla is kicking ass in her classes and has no need to be talking to a teacher after class.

"You sure you're okay?" Carter's face is serious. "Are the Lokarian cadets giving you a hard time?"

I shake my head. Since we were assigned to work together in flight class, we've become friends. He reminds me a little of my brothers, without all the merciless teasing and rough-housing, and it's nice to have a guy friend. My female suite mates are great, but I've always hung around men, so it feels totally natural to talk to Carter.

"It's nothing." I glance back at the tablet in my hands. "Just that the entire reason I came here is to learn Lokarian pods, and it's the one thing I haven't done."

Carter knows a little about my hoverbike experience—and he'd already heard about me hijacking a pod for an unauthorized joy ride—but nothing about me throwing myself at Koran. I haven't breathed a word of that to anyone. It's too humiliating. Not to mention the fact that it would probably earn me a one-way ticket back to Earth.

"Why don't you come with me to my private session this afternoon?"

"It's called private for a reason." I can imagine how shocked Koran would be if I showed up with Carter, and I'm pretty sure it would be obvious to anyone with eyes that something is going on. Although, nothing is going on. Not anymore, and not that it ever really was.

It was a momentary slip. That's what I've been telling myself since I stumbled back to my room, with my lips still puffy from his kiss and my heart still hammering wildly. I'd gotten caught up in the heat of the argument and acted on my impulses. Not that I hadn't done that before, but before there was always someone to stop me or drag the guy away or remind him that I was off-limits. Here there was no one to run interference, which was probably a very bad thing.

"You shouldn't miss out on learning just because the pod instructor doesn't like you." Carter taps his fingers across the glossy black console of the ship. "I know he's a bit gruff, but you can't let him intimidate you."

I think about the big Lokarian and his gold tattoos glinting in the dark garage, and his dark eyes flashing with heat. He doesn't intimidate me. He makes me want to crawl up him like a spider monkey. I give my head a small shake to clear that image and stop myself from thinking about bananas. Not to mention what I felt when he'd pressed between my legs. Heat rushes south, and I shift in my seat. "Jeez, Brooke."

He swivels his head to me. "What?"

"You're right," I tell him, as I study the readouts on my tablet and ignore his curious glance.

And he is. I *do* need to put my attraction aside and focus on work. Racing has always been a decent substitute for sexual release—and having such a powerful engine roaring between my legs might have spoiled me for most men—so getting back on a pod has to be the answer to forgetting what happened with Koran.

He grins. "So, you're coming with me?"

"No. I'm not going to ruin your private lesson. But I am going to talk to the jerk and find some way to work with him." I raise an eyebrow. "Otherwise, how can I ever get the chance to race you and see what you've got, cadet?"

"There she is." Carter winks at me. "That's the stalker I know."

I jab him with my elbow. "For the hundredth time, I was not stalking you. *You* were following me."

"By walking in front?"

We're both laughing when an alarm sounds on the hangar bay.

Carter leans forward and peers out the front view screen as red lights flash all around us. "You think this is for real, or just a drill?"

"Do Lokarians do drills?"

"Good point. We'd better at least check it out, since neither of us can operate this thing well enough to fly us out of a fire."

We walk down the ramp of the bomber, joining the rest of the flight class as sirens blare overhead and flashing lights make everyone appear tinted red. A group of Lokarian cadets stand in a huddle with their heads together, and I recognize a couple from my first pod class. I spin around so that my back is to them, moving closer to Carter.

"Any idea what's going on?" A human cadet with short, strawberry-blonde hair sidles up to us and yells over the noise.

I shake my head, forgetting her name and her military branch. I notice that her gaze is lingering on Carter, even though he doesn't seem to be paying attention to her. Before I can somehow communicate to him that he might have an admirer, Captain Kulvar strides over. A scowl dominates his face, and his hands are clenched together behind his back.

"Systems malfunction," he says. "Nothing serious."

I exchange a look with Carter. If it's nothing serious, why does the alien warrior look so tense? I think back to our first day in class and the biometric scanners that wouldn't work.

Carter leans close to my ear. "I thought these guys were supposed to be way more sophisticated in their technology than humans."

"Same." I notice the blonde watching us and put some distance between Carter and myself. I don't want her getting the wrong idea about us. I've dealt with my fair share of jealous women in the past, and I want nothing to do with that drama here. I'm relieved when a Lokarian cadet starts talking to her, distracting her from watching Carter, although I'm curious that the arrogant Lokarian from pod class would deign to talk to a human.

I shrug to myself. Better her than me. The pompous alien with jewelry adorning his arms is not my type, and she looks jittery as he looms over her. Just when I'm wondering if I should step in and help her out, the Lokarian walks off.

As I watch her hurry back into her assigned plane, I decide that she's not bad looking. I might just nudge my friend in her direction. Carter is definitely handsome, but he's not my type. Besides, we're better as friends, and I've never gotten anything but a buddy vibe off of him.

The alarms stop as suddenly as they'd started, the red flashes of light disappearing. Our instructor lets out a long breath and runs a hand through his short hair. "False alarm. Back to work. I want those diagnostic reports to me by the end of class, everyone."

Carter turns to return to our bomber, but I grab his sleeve. "What time is your private pod class today?"

"Right after dinner. I don't think the instructor eats or sleeps." He angles his head at me. "Why?"

"I want to make sure he's there when I go talk to him about putting me back in the advanced class." I step out of the way to let a group of Lokarian cadets pass us.

"Like I said." Carter starts up the ramp of the bomber and pauses to wait for me. "I don't think the guy ever leaves that garage."

I follow him back inside the bomber, and we resume running the diagnostic report. Now that I've decided to talk to Koran, I feel better. I've probably been making a big deal over nothing. I'll bet the kiss wasn't even a big deal to him. I don't know much about Lokarians, but I can't imagine the huge, gorgeous aliens have any problems getting females to fall at their feet. I'm sure he has tons of experience with women, and has kissed way more people than I have. I might have been his first human and maybe his first cadet, which would explain why he'd been so freaked out.

All I need to do is tell him it was a mistake—my mistake—and promise that it will never happen again. I can manage not to molest him while he teaches me, right? My mouth goes dry as I think about him again. Okay, better not to think about him.

Carter pushes a series of buttons, and I check the readout, twisting my head to look at him. "What's your opinion on strawberry-blondes?"

CHAPTER FOURTEEN

Brooke

"This is the right thing to do," I repeat to myself, as I walk across the campus toward the pod garage. Glancing back over my shoulder, I see the domes of the various buildings illuminated against the midnight-blue sky, and the mirrored structures reflecting the glow of the moons.

Lokar doesn't seem to have the same temperature fluctuations as Earth—it's never too hot or too cold, and I have no clue if they have seasons like we do—but there is no sun now to warm my bare arms as I walk. I shiver and cross my arms over my chest.

I meant to be at the garage earlier, but I'd gotten caught up in a friendly debate with my suite mates over which Lokarian instructor was toughest—Autumn insisted it's the hand-to-hand combat guy, but Layla made a pretty convincing argument that the shooting instructor is less forgiving. We were laughing so hard—and teasing Autumn by using as many creative curse words as we could think of—that I'd lost track of time. I'm still adjusting to having female friends, but it's actually nice having women I can talk to.

I hurry along the path, the paving stones lighting up as I step on them. I'm a little creeped out that I'm the only one walking outside, and I wish there was some other noise than that of my quick footsteps. I'd hoped to at least see Carter as he was leaving his private class, but I suspect he's long gone by now. I only hope Koran hasn't left for the night.

I just need to talk to him, I remind myself. I'll clear the air, and we can go back to annoying each other and maybe he can teach me something.

I round the corner and spot the low, wide dome of the pod garage. My heart sinks. There are no lights on inside, at least none that I can see.

Shit. I slow my pace. He must have gone for the night. I know where his quarters are, but no way am I going back there. I'm not sure if I trust him, and I *definitely* don't trust myself.

I walk closer to the entrance to the garage, but it appears to be closed. I hate to go another day without making any progress in my specialty, but I guess I'll have to track him down tomorrow. Letting out an impatient breath, I turn to walk back the way I came but I almost scream when I see three tall Lokarians blocking my path.

At first I think it might be Koran, but I quickly realize that it's not him. The cadets in front of me aren't nearly as broad as he is, and none of them share his gold markings. I do see the flash of metallic bands around their wrists and recognize one of the Lokarians from my flight class and my original advanced pod class.

"You shouldn't be out here by yourself, little human." The cadet I recognize eyes me up and down.

It only takes a second for me to realize that they are not here by accident. Fear prickles the back of my neck as their eyes roam my body without apology, but I pull myself up to my full height and square my shoulders. "I have a meeting."

One of them lets out a strangled laugh. "Trying to impress the Vratvos?"

I don't know what he means, so I ignore him. "I guess I'll see you guys in class." I attempt to walk around them, but they side-step to block me again.

"Not so fast." He puts a hand on my waist to keep me from moving.

My throat is thick, and my heart is pounding so hard I'm sure they can hear it. My first instinct is to yell for my brothers, but I know they can't save me now, and it hits me just how far from home and alone I am.

"She's not so fast when she's not on a pod," another mutters.

They all laugh, but the sound sends a shiver down my arms.

"Well, let's see." The one holding me drops his hand and holds his palms up as if in surrender. He jerks his head to one side. "Go ahead, human. Run."

I know I shouldn't take their bait, but I have to get away from these assholes. I dart to the side, but one of their legs shoots out and trips me, making me sprawl onto the paving stones that illuminate from the pressure. My hands and knees hit hard, sending pain arrowing up my arms and legs. Even though my palms burn, and I know they're bleeding, I try to push myself up. A heavy weight forces me back down and all the breath whooshes out of me.

His hot breath is on my neck as his large body crushes me. "Not so fast, after all, are you?"

I want to ram my elbow into him, but I can't move. He's so fucking heavy I can barely draw a breath. When he grinds something hard and huge into my ass, I rear my head back, catching him in the chin. He curses as he loosens his grip. I know I'm not going to get away from them, but no way am I going down without a fight.

Fingers dig into my hair and pull. "*Vlakking* human."

I grit my teeth from the pain, but then the hand is gone, and the weight is lifted from my back. Grunts and scuffling noises are met with screams and the sound of flesh hitting flesh. Are they fighting each other?

I don't wait to find out, but start trying to crawl away, even as my hands and knees burn.

"Brooke." The deep rumble of a voice makes me stop and look back.

Koran stands over the three cadets, who are doubled over and rolling around in obvious agony. He's heaving in labored breaths as he steps over them and scoops me into his arms. I wince, and his eyebrows press together.

"Is anything broken?"

I shake my head, unable to speak.

He nods once and starts walking toward the garage, giving a final, hard kick at one of the Lokarians on the ground. After he's pushed through the door, he strides past all the pods in the dark and opens another door into a small room that appears to be a combination office/workshop. He sits me on a high table and begins examining my bloodied palms.

Even with me sitting on a table, he still looms over me, but I'm not afraid. His touch is so gentle as he uncurls my hands that tears blur my vision. I try to blink them away. Since when do I cry?

"I'm okay." My voice breaks, revealing my lie.

He merely grunts in response, not looking up as he inspects my bruised elbows, his callused hands brushing over my skin. "What were you doing outside by yourself?"

"Technically, I wasn't by myself."

He gives me a stern look. "You should not walk around alone at night."

"How about those assholes shouldn't attack women?" I snap at him. "How about that wasn't my fault?"

"I did not say it was."

"Sure sounded like you were blaming the victim to me." More tears sting the backs of my eyes and one escapes out of the corner of my eye. "I shouldn't have to worry about walking around campus without getting mauled by fellow cadets. What the fuck kind of school is this?"

He raises his head, brushing the tear off my cheek with his thumb. "They will be punished."

My eyes flick to the door and beyond to where I imagine the cadets are still nursing their wounds on the ground. "You mean more than what you already did to them?"

His eyes lock on mine. "Much more."

I take a shaky breath. "You know I was actually looking for you, so I guess it's a good thing you found me. I mean, obviously it was a good thing you found me."

One of his dark eyebrows lifts. "You were looking for me? Why?"

I shrug. "I thought I should make things right. I thought I could apologize and talk you into teaching me." I take a quick breath and barrel through my prepared speech, even though his eyes bore into me. "I know I shouldn't have kissed you, and I know it freaked you out. I don't know what I was thinking, but if we both admit it was a huge mistake and promise never to mention it again, maybe we can do a hard reset."

I gasp for breath and lift my gaze to his.

His eyes are molten. "A hard reset?"

I nod eagerly, trying not to notice that my pulse is fluttering. "We start over and forget everything that's happened. What do you think? Is it a deal?"

Koran cups my face in one hand as he drags his thumb across my bottom lip. "What if I don't want to forget?"

CHAPTER FIFTEEN

Koran

I hold her face and watch her pupils flare with desire. Her pulse is thumping rapidly in her neck and her breath is quick.

"What do you mean you don't want to—?" she starts to ask.

I cover her lips with my thumb. "I mean, no deal. I don't want to forget kissing you."

She inhales sharply, and I move my thumb from her mouth to her jawline, tipping her face up to mine.

"But you said..." A crease forms between her eyes. "I thought you didn't want to... You're my instructor."

She's right about all of this, but I don't care. After seeing that Lokarian cadet on top of her, I know one thing above all else. Brooke is mine. Mine to protect, and mine to claim. I've known it deep within myself since the first moment I laid eyes on her, but I tried to suppress my desire. Now, I don't want to. My primal desire to mark this human as mine is raging, and I need to take her before I go mad.

"I will still teach you," I husk. "But I need more than that. I need you." I drag one finger down her throat and past her collarbone, feeling her heart hammering. "I think you want me, too."

She nods without uttering a word, a small gasp escaping her lips.

That is all I need before crashing my mouth to hers. Her lips open to me and I tangle my tongue with hers, savoring the sweetness of her. I move my hands around to her back then down, grasping her ass cheeks and jerking her to me. Her legs open and straddle my waist as I lean against the table, our bodies flush.

Her moans grow louder, filling the workshop and startling me. For a small creature, she is loud. But I like her noises and the hum of her throat as she groans into my mouth.

Brooke runs both hands through my hair, tightening her grip until it almost hurts as she holds my head to her and kisses me harder.

This human female is nothing like I expected of her race, and nothing like her small stature would suggest. Although I've seen hints of heat from her before, I am not prepared for her fiery response.

I growl as she moves eagerly against me. I need to protect her and make her mine. No one will hurt her again. No one will touch her but me. I slide my hands up her body, my fingers skimming the soft swell of her breasts. My blood is a roar in my ears, as my swollen cock presses hard against my pants.

Tearing her mouth from mine, she gazes up at me, her chest heaving as she fumbles with my shirt. She yanks it out of my pants, and I lift my arms so she can get it over my head. Once she's tossed my shirt to the floor, she drags her fingernails down my chest.

"You're so..." Her gaze moves from my bare chest muscles up to my eyes.

I force myself to take even breaths. "Yes?"

She bites her lower lip, her trembling fingers brushing across my skin as she moves her hands down to my stomach muscles. "You're bigger than a human guy. And harder. It's like you're solid muscle."

I close my hand over her shaking one. "Are you afraid I will hurt you?" I turn her hands around in mine and bring her scratched palms to my lips, kissing them. "I will never hurt you, Brooke. I am not like those other Lokarians."

"I know." She bobs her head up and down. "But I've never...I mean, this would be my first..."

I wait for her to finish, but her words trail off and her gaze drops to the floor. Then I realize what she means. She is untouched. She has never been claimed by a male before.

My heart swells with a rush of affection and an even more urgent need to shield this female from males. Including myself.

I step back and her legs fall from my waist. "We should not."

She frowns at me, her breathing still heavy. "Oh, we definitely should."

I press my lips together. "You do not know—"

"You're going to really need to stop telling me what I know and what I want." She locks eyes with me as she hops down off the table. "I may have never been with a guy before, but that doesn't mean I don't know what I want. And I want you, Koran. Right here and right now."

She unfastens her pants and shimmies out of them until they are pooled around her feet. She kicks them over to the corner with my shirt. My mouth goes dry as she whips her shirt over her head in a single motion, tossing that aside, as well. Then Brooke is standing in front of me in nothing but sheer, black fabric covering her breasts, and a wisp of the same black cloth between her legs.

I cannot speak or move as she hops back up on the table and spreads her legs. "So, are you going to fuck me or not, Koran?"

Her words are a jolt that make me move quickly to her, jerking her body flush to mine and crushing my lips to hers. Our kiss is hard and deep, both of us rocking against each other.

My cock strains and aches as I grind between her open legs. She tugs roughly at my pants, finally unfastening them and forcing them down. Then she's freed my cock from the tight boxer briefs that keep me in place when I ride and is holding it in one hand.

Her small fingers squeezing my shaft make my eyes roll back into my head. "*Vlak,* Brooke," I say when I tear my mouth from hers. If she keeps this up I will not last long enough to fuck her. It has been too long since a female has touched me, and the sensations are almost overwhelming.

She glances down at where her hand strokes up and down, licking her lips and grinning. "Don't you like this?"

"Too much." I kiss my way down her neck and chest. I nip at each firm nipple through the see-through fabric, sucking until it is hard and pebbled before moving down even farther.

She gasps as I push her down onto her back and nestle my face between her legs. I slide my hands under her ass cheeks and open her legs wider, my cock getting even harder at the sight of the sheer, black fabric barely covering her sex.

I use my tongue to move the fabric to one side, dragging it up the length of her soft pink folds and tasting her slickness. "You're soaked for me already."

She moans and writhes beneath my touch, her hips arching up as I find her swollen nub and start to circle it with the tip of my tongue.

Brooke tangles her fingers in my hair as I work her with my tongue, sucking and flicking until her breath is ragged and her moans are deep and throaty.

"Your beard," she gasps. "It feels so good."

I move my face gently from side to side, scraping my scruff against her wetness.

She arches her back and digs her nails into my scalp, lifting her knees high. "Fuck, yes, Koran."

I register her fingernails in my flesh, but barely notice the pain. I'm too caught up in her hips moving up to meet me and the small keening noises she's making. When she starts to buck up, I keep licking her until her entire body is jerking and trembling, her fingers like claws as she holds my head between her legs and comes on my tongue.

She sags back on the table, her legs shaking, and I stand, ripping the black fabric between her legs all the way off. My cock juts out from my body, and I notch it at her wet opening.

Brooke props herself up on her elbows and her hungry gaze meets mine. "Yes, Koran."

CHAPTER SIXTEEN

Brooke

My breath hitches in my chest as I watch him hesitate, the thick crown of his cock slick. I can't help staring at him. Not only is he the first guy I've gotten the chance to really look at fully naked, he's the first alien I've ever seen without clothes.

Even though Lokarian males look like a bigger, more-ripped version of humans in their badass military uniforms, they don't look exactly like humans *everywhere*. For starters, they don't have testicles. Since I've never thought hairy balls were exactly appealing, I don't mind their absence, and I guess the Lokarians evolved to have their most sensitive bits inside them.

When I held his cock earlier, I'd felt the bumpy texture I can now see on his shaft. The broad head is smooth, but the rest looks almost like some kind of sex toy designed to give extra friction. Ribbed, I think is the term. I might be a virgin, but I've heard my brothers talk about sex enough when they thought I wasn't around. I eye Koran's cock, both eager to feel it inside me, and nervous that it might split me in two.

"Brooke?" He leans over me and strokes a hand down my face. "Are you sure?"

I wiggle my hips to take the top of his crown, already feeling the stretch. "I want this."

He pushes in slowly, his gaze locked on mine and our faces so close that his breath is warm on my cheek.

"I don't want it slow." I reach my arms around his back, my fingers slipping on his skin. "I don't like anything slow. Fuck me hard, Koran."

He doesn't ask me again, driving all the way into me with a final powerful thrust. He burrows his head in my neck as he holds himself inside me.

All the air leaves my body, and I dig my fingers into his hard flesh, gasping. Maybe I spoke too soon, I think. I never imagined he could be so deep inside me that it's like he's a part of me.

The sharp sting fades, and there is only the wonderful fullness of his cock. I squeeze my legs around his waist as he groans. I know he's giving me time to adjust, but I want more. I want to feel those ridges. "You can move. I won't break."

He lifts his head from my neck, holding my gaze with his own molten one, as he drags his cock out. It's only then that I fully appreciate his textured shaft, my eyelids fluttering as it rubs me in all the right ways.

"You're sure I'm not hurting you?" he grits out, his jaw tight.

"I'm sure."

He thrusts back in me, making me moan. Even though I've never been fucked before, my body seems to know what to do, and I instinctively move with him. I see sweat beading along his brow.

"Are you okay?" I ask.

He nods, but his voice is strained. "You're so small. So tight."

I slide my hands down to his ass and jerk him back inside

me, angling my hips up to meet the thrust. "That doesn't mean I don't want you to fuck me hard."

He mutters a Lokarian curse as he strokes into me again and again, skin slapping against skin.

This is better than I imagined it would be, and I've had lots of time to fantasize about getting fucked. Of course, none of my fantasies included an alien with a massive, ribbed cock.

I'm panting when he rears back, scooping me up and standing without stopping his pace. He moves me up and down his cock as he stands, and I put my hands on his shoulders to brace myself even though they're slippery with sweat.

The muscles in his neck are taut, and he looks down at where our bodies meet, moaning.

"You like watching yourself fuck me?" I say and watch his eyes widen.

"You're stretched so pretty around my cock, I could watch you ride me all night."

I lean closer and run my tongue around his ear lobe. "Now I have a new favorite thing to ride. Your cock feels even better than an engine between my legs."

"And your tight little cunt is the best thing I've ever felt in my life."

For some reason, I love hearing the word cunt roll off his tongue. I give his ear a hard nip and then crush my mouth to his. Our tongues battle as sensations storm through me—fiery and raw. Everything about him feels so good and so right. I don't care about anything in the moment but the feel of him inside me.

He takes a few steps back as we kiss, and then drops into a chair, his hands clamping tighter on my hips as he moves me up and down. I put my hands on his hard pec muscles and lean into him, tilting my hips forward and rubbing my clit against him.

His eyes are dark and hungry as he watches me, never taking his scorching gaze off me as liquid heat builds in my core. My ragged breath becomes desperate pants as I begin to come again, the ripples of pleasure rocking me. I scream as my body clenches around his cock over and over.

Then Koran's fingers are biting into my flesh as he hammers me down onto him, and I swear his cock gets even harder and bigger as he explodes inside me, arching his head back and roaring with his release.

I slump down onto him, my body damp against his and our chests rising and falling together. He slides his hands from my hips to my back and holds me tight to him.

"Are you okay?" he asks, after a few minutes of nothing but the sounds of our heavy breathing.

I kiss his chest, tracing one finger along a thick, gold line swirling across his bronze skin. "Oh, I'm a lot better than okay."

He laughs softly, running a hand through my hair and smoothing a few damp strands off my forehead. "Yes, you are."

I swat at his chest, but I'm pleased he wasn't disappointed. I hate being a newbie at anything, and I would hate to be bad at *this*.

His hand strokes my back. "You are sure I did not hurt you? It was not too rough for your first time?"

I lift my head to meet his eyes. "I didn't say it didn't hurt." He flinches, but I put a hand on his chest. "But it was a good hurt. And then it felt amazing."

He smiles, pulling me in for a kiss. "You were amazing. I never imagined humans would be so…"

I grin as he lets his words trail off and color fills his cheeks. "So, I'm your first human?"

His eyebrows lift. "Of course."

"I guess this bunch of cadets are the first humans to set foot on your planet, right?"

"Aside from some human military advisors, yes. But none of them had nearly the ass that you do, especially since they were all males."

I pretend to scowl at him. "I wonder if we're the first Lokarian and human to ever…" I suck in a breath as panic flutters in my chest. "I totally forgot about birth control. I'm not on anything since I've never…and I didn't expect to… You don't think I can get pregnant, do you? No offense, but a baby is definitely not in my short-term plans."

He grins. "Don't worry. All Lokarians get contraceptive shots. We only stop getting them when we are ready to procreate."

I let out a deep sigh. "So, there's no way you can knock me up? Oh, thank God. Again, no offense."

"None taken." He cups my face in his hand. "But I never would have put you at risk if it had not been safe."

Not what I would have expected from the tough Lokarian, but I like it. "Thanks, Koran." I twist around and spot my clothes bunched on the floor. "I guess I should get dressed."

He does not let go of me. "I don't know. I think I prefer you like this."

I glance down at his glistening chest and the heavy, gold tattoos. "I like this view of you, too, but I need to get back to my dorm before my suite mates send out a search party."

He circles his arms around me tighter, hugging me close for a moment, the thrumming of his heartbeat steady. I could easily fall asleep just like this, with his strong arms holding me and his broad chest warming me. But I can't. I need to leave before I end up spending the night and having a lot of explaining to do.

I push away from him. "Koran?"

"I like hearing my name on your lips," he murmurs to me, his words a caress as they skate down my spine.

I like being held by this alien way more than I want to admit. And way more than I should considering that he's my teacher and officially off-limits. "I really need to go."

He holds me for another long moment before loosening his arms. "And I need to see you again." He sits up, his arms cradling my back to keep me from falling. "Will you come back tomorrow night?"

I cock my head at him. The heat in his eyes has been replaced by something softer, a tenderness that makes my pulse skitter. Having a fling with a teacher is one thing. Falling for one is quite another. "Are you going to teach me or fuck me?"

He growls low, the fire returning to his dark gaze. "Both. First we will ride pods, then I will ride you."

A thrill ricochets through my body. "Deal."

CHAPTER SEVENTEEN

Brooke

"So, are you going to spill it or what?" Autumn asks me the next morning, as we're walking across campus to class. Elena and Layla have gone ahead to their weapons training, but we both have a lecture on Skrum technology in the main building.

I glance over at her quickly, hoping my cheeks don't look as pink as they feel. "Spill what?"

Autumn stifles a laugh. "Girl, you snuck in late last night and took a shower. And you've been humming all morning. All I want to know is which cadet you got it on with?" She drops her voice to a conspiratorial whisper. "Is it one of the Lokarians? Or is it that cute Naval officer you were talking to at dinner?"

"Carter?" I shake my head hard. "No way. We're just friends. And why do you assume I got it on? I told you I was taking a late-night pod class."

"With the instructor you hate?" She makes a face. "Your good mood is definitely not because of that jerk."

I feel an urge to defend Koran and tell my friend that he isn't the jerk I thought he was, but I know I should keep what happened between us a secret. I trust Autumn more than anyone else at the academy, but I also know that any whisper of something between me and a Lokarian instructor would have me on the first spaceship back to Earth.

A tall, Lokarian instructor strides by us in his snug black uniform, his boots thumping on the wide paving stones. His brown hair curls around collar of his jacket, and silver tattoos flash through it as they swirl up back of his neck. Autumn and I both go quiet until he passes.

"I'm telling you, I really love riding pods," I say, when the alien is far enough away not to hear us, tightening my high ponytail with both hands.

She gives me a sidelong glance, but shrugs. "Whatever you say, but I know the look of someone who got some when I see it." She points a finger at me and waves it up and down. "And you, my friend, have that look."

"What look?" Carter comes up behind us, walking quickly.

"Don't do that." I put a hand to my chest as Autumn jumps. "You scared us half to death."

He grins, giving Autumn a wave across me. "Sorry. I wanted to catch you before you got inside. Are you heading to the Skrum lecture?"

I nod and tuck a loose strand of hair back into my ponytail. "You?"

"Yep." His gaze widens as it locks on my hands. "What happened to you?"

I've almost forgotten the scrapes on my palms from the night before. Koran had applied some salve to them after we'd gotten dressed, and the Lokarian concoction did a pretty good job of healing them, so now only small abrasions remain. "It's nothing. I tripped."

Autumn eyes them, then shifts her suspicious gaze to me, but doesn't say anything. Instead, she focuses on Carter. "Brooke tells me you two have the same flight class."

"That's right. We were assigned to a bomber together."

"Really?" Autumn's eyebrows rise. "So, you're partners?"

I know where she's going with this, but I decide not to correct her. If the woman is hell-bent on thinking I'm hooking up with the clean-cut Naval officer, far be it from me to continue to talk her out of it. Besides, the more she's convinced I'm banging him, the less chance she'll find out I screwed one of my instructors.

Carter jerks a thumb at me. "This one has good instincts for ships."

Autumn gives him what could only be called a "no, duh" look. "It doesn't hurt that she grew up working in a garage back home."

Carter eyes me. "You never told me that." He nudges me playfully. "I thought we were friends. What else are you holding out on me, Butler?"

"Probably not much," Autumn mutters so only I can hear her.

We reach the glass front of the building, walking under the massive, metal arch and through the wide doors. Carter lets us walk in first, even though the doors are holographic and there's nothing to hold open. It reminds me of men in the South—the ones that were raised right, as my father would say—and I smile at him. I may not be attracted to Carter, but he might not be a bad option for Autumn.

"How'd it go with the pod instructor last night?" He asks as we make our way to a staircase that curves up one side of the foyer.

I almost trip over my own feet, and he catches me by the elbow.

"The pod instructor?" I ask, my voice quavering.

He angles his head at me. "Yeah, weren't you going to talk to him about getting back in the advanced class?"

"Right. Of course. I thought I'd see you there, but I ended up going later than I'd planned." The words rush out of me in a fast jumble. "Then when I finally did leave the dorm, it was dark and no one else was out, and he wasn't there."

"That's too bad," Carter says. "I would have put good money on the guy sleeping in his garage."

Sleeping wasn't exactly what we'd done, but Carter was right that Koran had been there, even though the lights had been off.

I shrug as we start walking up the stairs three across and ignore the curious looks Autumn is giving me. "It's fine. I'm sure I can talk with him later."

"I still think you should come to my class. I'll put in a good word for you. The guy seems to like me."

Not as much as he likes me, I think. "Maybe I will. Thanks."

We reach the next level, and Carter directs us across one of the walkways suspended over the lobby, and down a long corridor.

"How do you know this place so well?" Autumn asks. "It's still like a maze to me."

"Are you guys going to the Skrum lecture?" A woman's voice calls out from behind.

When I turn, I see that it's the strawberry blonde from flight class. The only other female, and the one who I'd sworn had been checking out Carter.

"We are." He stops to let her catch up to us.

She gives him a wide smile and flicks her fingers through her short hair, barely looking at me or Autumn. "Great. I'm totally lost."

She manages to step between me and Carter as we continue down the hall. Well, I was right about her. She's definitely into him.

"I'm Cassie," she says, mostly to Carter, but Autumn and I

introduce ourselves anyway. She smiles at us but pivots right back to Carter.

I try not to be annoyed. It's not like *I'm* into Carter, but I am a bit territorial about him. After all, he is my friend and partner in flight class.

Autumn nudges me and rolls her eyes as the woman laughs loudly at something Carter said that wasn't remotely funny. I press my lips together to keep from laughing out loud and nudge Autumn back.

We finally reach an open set of doors and Carter lets us all walk in first. The lecture hall is large and dimly lit, with curved rows of seats descending to a small stage positioned in front of a massive screen. Most of the seats are already filled—clearly not everyone had a hard time finding the lecture hall—so we slip into two sets of two seats each at the back, with Carter and Cassie behind us.

Autumn takes out her tablet. "Ready to learn about the horrific alien swarm that wants to destroy our planet?"

Cassie lets out a stream of exaggerated giggles behind us, and Autumn and I both put a hand over our mouths to keep from laughing.

"I think I might take the Skrum over this," I whisper to her, motioning behind us with my eyes.

"Agreed," she mouths, as a Lokarian stomps onto the stage with his arms clasped behind his back.

I recognize him as the silver fox alien who'd welcomed us on the first day. He doesn't bother with a microphone, his booming voice carrying through the hall easily. "As most of you already know, I am Commander Daryx, the head of the Lokarian Warrior Academy."

He strides back and forth across the stage as he talks, a single braid down one side of his hair swinging as he turns. "What you don't know is why you're here today."

Murmurs pass through the room like a muffled wave.

"I am here to talk about the Skrum, and how imperative it is that we train you to defeat them, yes. But more than that, I am here to tell you that we suspect the Skrum are currently engaged in sabotage against this very academy."

The murmurs become an angry buzz as everyone exchanges glances.

The academy head spins to face us. "And we believe the Skrum have the help of a mole within our ranks."

CHAPTER EIGHTEEN

Koran

The campus hums with the news of a traitor in our ranks. I was not in the room where Daryx announced the traitor, but it is all anyone is talking about. Even now, as the cadets in my advanced class dismount their pods after racing the track, they talk about it.

"It could only be a human." One of the Lokarian cadets disengages his energy helmet and unhooks the device from his ear.

"How could a human be working with the Skrum?" Another shakes his head as he swings his big body off the back of the shiny vehicle. "They didn't know the creatures existed until we told them, and that wasn't long ago."

The original speaker mumbles something dark and angry about Earthlings.

"You friend is right." A human cadet hops off a pod, landing effortlessly on the ground. "We don't have the history with the

Skrum that you do. Besides, it's our planet they're after. Why would any human help them? Or know how to?"

All the Lokarian cadets turn to face him. Even though what he says makes sense, it's clear they do not wish to hear it.

"Why should we trust you, human?"

The cadet shrugs. "Maybe because I traveled halfway across the galaxy to train to fight against your enemy."

The Lokarians grumble and shift, shooting him murderous looks. Although I admire the human cadet's guts, I do not wish to referee a fight in my class.

"The Skrum are both our enemy now." I step between the human cadet I remember is called Carter, and the Lokarians. "We should concentrate on fighting them, not each other." I narrow my gaze at all the cadets. "Agreed?"

They all reluctantly nod and mutter their agreement.

"Class dismissed," I tell them, turning and heading back to my office, grateful the day is over.

"Sir?"

Carter's voice makes me stop and turn. I have been impressed by the Naval officer's ability on pods and how quickly his skill level has advanced—especially since I gave him a couple of private classes—but I am in no mood to coach him privately tonight. "If you were looking for additional instruction, I'm afraid—"

"No, sir." He waves a hand. "That's not it. I was actually going to talk to you about a friend of mine who wants to get into your advanced class."

Now he has my attention. Any human cadet who showed promise is already in my advanced class, so I cannot imagine who he means. "A friend? A human?"

His mouth twitches up. "Yes, a human. A woman, actually."

My pulse quickens. He can't mean Brooke, can he? I eye this human with short, light hair and blue eyes much like Brooke's. He is nowhere near as large as me, but his arms are roped with muscle and his stomach is corded, both things I know females desire.

"This woman is good on pods?" I ask, crossing my arms over my chest. Maybe he means someone else, and the jealous flutter in my stomach is for nothing.

He nods. "Very good. She wanted to come talk to you about getting back in the advanced class, but I thought I'd put in a good word for her, first."

I grunt. "It sounds like you are a very good friend. You know this woman from Earth?"

A quick shake of his head. "No. We just met here, but we *are* good friends, and I can vouch for her, sir."

The thought of the female I claimed last night being close to another male—this human male with the easy smile—makes me grit my teeth. "Her name?"

"Cadet Butler."

I twist my neck quickly so that it cracks, and Carter's smile wavers. The device in my pocket buzzes, and I retrieve it, grateful for the escape, although not grateful when I see a message from my clan leader flash onto the small screen.

I frown and glance up at Carter. "I'll take your words under advisement, cadet. Now I need to read an incoming transmission."

I spin on my heel and leave him, staring down at the message as I walk.

Vlak. Glatzor wants a progress report, and I have nothing to give him. I enter my office and cross to the worktable where I'd spread Brooke out the night before. I brace my hands on the edge of the high table, squeezing the hard surface in frustration.

I had already been reticent to do what my clan leader wanted, and that had been before the head of the Lokarian academy had announced the existence of a Skrum spy. No way can I carry out any sort of illicit mission to gather intel on new technology. Not with the campus on high alert.

I drag in a breath and let it out, closing my eyes and convincing myself that none of this has anything to do with me. It isn't possible that the traitor getting information for the Skrum is Glatzor, is it?

I give my head a brutal shake and slam a palm onto the table, welcoming the sharp sting of pain that shoots up my arm. No. Impossible. Clan Vratvos might be involved in questionable activities, but we would never work in tandem with our planet's enemy. Not for any reward. Right?

I think of my clan leader and his rough, scarred face. He reached the level of leader by killing most in his path and surviving many attempts on his own life. He is ruthless and feared, but he is no traitor to his people. No Lokarian would betray their kind.

But then I think back to what Carter said. Why would the traitor be a human? They were unaware of the Skrum until recently, and they have never encountered them. How would a human even know how to make contact with the alien swarm?

Then that means the traitor has to be a Lokarian. This thought makes me sick, and I swallow down the bitter taste of bile in my throat. Even worse than a Lokarian being the mole would be if I was part of this betrayal. Although I have not given Glatzor any information, I have been quietly compiling it.

My gaze darts to the metal cabinet against the wall. I cannot know for sure that clan Vratvos is not aligned with the Skrum, so I must destroy any information I gathered for them. I'm very aware that this information could also be used to make a case that I am the Skrum mole.

Crossing to the cabinet, I throw open the doors and reach into the back, wrapping my fingers around a small, metal device. I pull it out and peer at it in my palm. It's so small, it's almost difficult to believe that I've been able to record conversations and photograph documents with a touch of a button.

"No more." I stride back to the table and place the flat, metal cylinder on the surface. I search the room and settle on a heavy pod wrench, snatching it off the wall and bringing it down on the device. The crunch of metal is satisfying, and I do it again and again until there are only battered shards remaining.

When I stop, I'm breathing heavily, and I see that the table has several grooves in it from my powerful blows.

"I don't know what that table did to piss you off, but remind me not to do it."

I whirl around and see Brooke standing in the doorway, her hands on her hips and a smirk on her face.

"What are you doing here?" I ask, before I can think to measure my voice.

She looks startled, her eyes going to the crushed device and then back to me. "I thought we were meeting after classes were over. You promised to teach me something before…" Her words drift off, and I can see the doubt washing over her face.

I drop the wrench and close the distance between us in a couple of long strides. I need her in my arms and to know that she is real and that she is mine. I sweep her into a hard embrace, my mouth crashing onto hers and my arms circling her and lifting her off the ground.

She makes a startled squeak, but then sinks into the kiss, opening her mouth to mine and pressing her body eagerly against me. When I pull away to catch my breath, she gazes up at me and blinks a few times. "I thought you said we'd ride pods first."

My hands move desperately down her body, savoring the soft curves on her lithe frame. The need to bury my aching cock inside her and forget everything wrong in my life is almost overpowering. "I lied."

CHAPTER NINETEEN

Brooke

His ferocity takes my breath away, but only for a moment. I need this, I think as his hand grips the back of my neck, tilting my head back so he can kiss me even harder. I can barely tell where his breath ends and mine begins as his tongue fights with mine, but I know it's his heart hammering against my chest as he holds me to him.

When he pulls away for a breath, his eyes are wild and his breath heaving. "Fuck, Brooke."

"That's kind of the point," I say, fumbling with his pants. "But first, I want to try something."

My hands tremble slightly as I slide his pants down, taking his black boxer briefs with them. His thick cock springs up, and as soon as I see it all hard and ribbed, I know I have to suck it.

Fucking isn't the only thing I'm new at. I've given a hand job here and there, but back in Texas, I was never left alone with a guy long enough to do more than that, even though I'd heard plenty of talk about sucking dick. Mostly from my brothers when they thought I wasn't within earshot, but it was still helpful information. Information I now plan to put to good use.

I fist the base of Koran's long cock and bend over, making him twitch in surprise.

"What are you...?" His words drift off as I wrap my lips around his crown.

I give him a hard suck, then pull my lips off him and look up. "You got to taste me. It's only fair I get to taste you."

He groans and tangles his fingers in my hair, his gaze darkening. This is all the encouragement I need. I turn my attention back to his cock, licking down one side and back the other before swirling my tongue around the head and taking it in my mouth.

His grip on my hair tightens as I take as much of him as I can in my mouth, squeezing when his crown bumps the back of my throat. If I thought he was big when he was stretching me, I definitely know he's huge now.

Koran makes a low rumbling sound when I pump my mouth up and down his shaft a few times, and I gaze up at him. His eyes are riveted to me, the expression on his face almost worshipful.

Even though I've never sucked a cock before, I love how powerful I feel with it filling my mouth, and I love that I can make his moans echo off the glass dome.

I pull back for a moment and give him a wicked grin. "You like the way I suck you?"

He squeezes his eyes closed for a brief second. "I've never seen anything as pretty as your mouth wrapped around my cock. Well, except for the sight of my cock splitting you."

"Not yet." I wave a finger at him. "First, I want you to come in my mouth."

"*Vlak,*" he says, his cock twitching.

I smile and circle my fingers around the base of him as I take him into my mouth again, pumping my hand while I move my mouth up and down, my lips bumping on his hard ridges. I remember how those ridges felt inside me, and a pulse of heat throbs between my legs. As much as I loved being fucked by Koran, I also love knowing that I can make him this crazy just with my mouth.

His fingers curl hard in my hair, and he pulls me into him as his cock starts to jerk. I don't stop moving, squeezing the base of his cock as his groans become louder. When he starts to come, I take him as far down the back of my throat as I can, swallowing his saltiness eagerly.

He lets out a deep breath, and I sit back, wiping the corners of my mouth and making a satisfied sound of my own. "Delicious."

Koran grabs my wrists and hoists me to my feet. "I hope you don't think I'm letting you leave without hearing your screams."

My breath catches as he lifts me onto the back of a pod. Consider me a big fan of Lokarian stamina.

CHAPTER TWENTY

Brooke

"I think I'm getting worse," Autumn says, as we walk out of our hand-to-hand combat class the next day. Her face is flushed, and she rubs one shoulder.

"No, you're not." I don't tell her it would be hard to get worse than she was when we started, or that the intense instructor doesn't seem impressed by either of us. I know the serious Lokarian scares the hell out of her, so I don't want to freak her out any more than she already is.

"You're just saying that, which I appreciate." She glances back at the door to the training studio. "But I'm going to have to do something, or I won't be passing this class, and I don't think I'd survive it a second time."

"What about talking to the instructor?"

"You mean like you talked to your pod teacher?" She grimaces. "We see how well that worked. You have to ride pods late at night. No way do I want to be practicing combat techniques after hours."

I don't admit to her that Koran and I do a lot more than riding pods. I'm just glad none of my suite mates have raised questions about me coming in late two nights in a row. As cool as the other women are, I'm not sure how they would react to the news that I'm sleeping with one of our teachers. I'm not sure what I would think if the situation was reversed. If I think about it too hard, I'm not sure what *I* think about it.

Logically, I know that I shouldn't be involved with an instructor, especially the pod instructor. I'm here to learn skills to help Earth battle a hideous alien swarm, which includes getting even better at riding pods. The last thing on my mind should be guys and even farther down the list should be Lokarians.

What is it about the tough alien that draws me to him? He's gruff and bossy and seems to think I need to be taken care of— none of those are things that should appeal to me. But every time he touches me or looks at me with those whiskey-colored eyes, I melt inside. It didn't hurt that he saved me from those asshole cadets. It also doesn't hurt that he knows exactly how to touch me to make my body ignite.

"Brooke?"

I realize that I just let out a deep sigh, and Autumn is staring at me with one eyebrow cocked. I shake my head. "Thinking about all my after-hours work, and how much it sucks."

"Oh." Autumn matches my faster pace as we walk down the white corridor. "I'll bet. Thanks for the suggestion, though. I don't know what I'd do if you weren't in the class with me."

We make our way down a curved staircase to one of the dining halls. I'm glad for the midday break, because the hand-to-hand combat class really gave me an appetite. We pause inside the long hall, with high ceilings and soaring windows at the end.

Shimmering chandeliers that look like starbursts hang down the length of the room over a single, long rectangular table that twists and turns to go up and down the space. Conversation is a low hum as rows of cadets fill the tables—black Lokarian uniforms interspersed with the dark-blue Earth ones.

Autumn waves her hand in the air. "There are Layla and Elena."

The two women are at the far end of the room. Layla's white-blonde hair makes them easy to spot, especially as it contrasts with Elena's nearly black braid.

We make our way through the crowded dining hall and around the twisted table until we reach them. They both scoot over so we can sit.

Autumn eyes the center of the table where plates of food move past on a continuous conveyer belt, plucking one and placing it in from of her. "Sorry we're late. Hand-to-hand."

Both women nod, knowing that this is Autumn's most challenging class, and that we usually end up the last ones to leave since we haven't mastered the move of the day.

"We had cryptography." Layla takes a bite of Lokarian sponge bread.

Autumn swirls a spoon in her stew. "Lucky."

Elena wrinkles her nose, making me think that she feels the same way about cryptography that Autumn feels about hand-to-hand. "Deciphering Lokarian and Skrum ciphers is not my idea of a good time."

I take a plate from the converter belt of food, recognizing the spicy meat that reminds me a little bit of pulled pork. "Have you heard anything more about the Skrum spy?" I keep my voice low, even though I suspect half the conversations in the room are about the very same thing.

Elena leans forward. "Nothing, and I've kept my ear to ground on this one."

The way she says it makes me wonder—not for the first time

—what her specialty really is, although whenever I've asked, she's said "intelligence" and left it at that.

"They must have some evidence." Layla says. "Otherwise they wouldn't make an announcement like that, right?"

"Unless they're trying to force the spy out into the open." Elena glances around us. "If the traitor thinks they're on to him —or her—they might do something that would give themselves away."

Autumn stops chewing. "Like what?"

"If it was me, I'd get busy destroying any evidence." Layla waves a flat piece of bread as she talks. "And I'd cover my tracks."

Autumn shakes her head. "I can't imagine anyone here working with the Skrum."

I tend to agree with her, peering down the length of the table. Everyone at the academy has joined their planet's military to fight against enemies, not help them. It doesn't make any sense. I see Carter sitting a few spaces down and catch his eye, giving him a small wave.

His face lights up when he sees me and he rises quickly, walking over to stand behind me. I swing my legs over the bench to face him. His smile falters, and he makes a jerking motion to the side with his head. "Can I talk to you for a second, Brooke?"

He never calls me by my first name. I nod and stand, moving over to the corner of the room with him even as my friends' gazes follow us. I know they probably think something's going on, and this definitely will do nothing to convince Autumn we're just friends.

"What's up?" I ask. "You okay?"

He leans close, taking my elbow in one hand and bending his head down to mine. "I know you didn't want me to, but I talked to the pod instructor about you getting back in the advanced class."

Heat fills my cheeks. "You didn't have to do that—"

He waves away my protests with his other hand, not releasing my elbow. "That's not what I wanted to tell you, although the guy did say he'd consider it."

"So, what did you want to tell me?"

"I want you to tell me I'm crazy." He darts a glance to one side, then drops his voice to a near whisper. "But I think the pod instructor might be the mole."

I try to pull away, but his grip on me is too firm. "What? No way." I realize that I've said that too loudly and a few cadets glance over. I steady my voice and suppress my irritation. "Why would you think that?"

Carter draws in a long breath. "When I was making my case for you, the guy got a message on his device."

I angle my head at him. "So? I'm sure a lot of Lokarians get messages on their devices. Don't they use those to communicate with each other?"

Carter gives me a withering look. "Don't you think I know that, Butler?"

I'm glad he's back to using my last name, but not thrilled by this conversation. "Okay, so explain why getting a message makes someone a spy for the Skrum."

"It wasn't that he got a message. It was what the message said."

My stomach tightened. "How would you know what a Lokarian message said?"

He relaxes his grip on my elbow, moving his hand up to my shoulder. "I'm Naval intelligence, specializing in linguistics." He pauses, as if to let this sink in. "I can read Lokarian."

I don't know if I want to know the answer, but I ask anyway. "So, what did it say?"

"Basically, whomever was messaging him was telling him they received the targets for the mission."

Shit. Am I really involved with the traitor? I shake my head, willing it not to be true. Koran couldn't betray his own people, could he? I don't want to believe it, but then again, how much do I really know the guy?

"Are you okay, Butler?" Carter puts an arm around me. "You look a little pale."

"It's just a shock," I manage to mutter. "That it could be a teacher."

"So, what should we do?"

CHAPTER TWENTY-ONE

Koran

Why is he touching her?

Blood pounds in my ears as I watch the cadet from my advanced class—Carter—put his arm around Brooke. He's talking low in her ear, and she's nodding.

What is he saying to her? What could the human male possibly have to tell her that would require him to be so close to her?

I'm rooted to the doorway of the cadet dining hall, and for a moment, I forget why I am there. I spent hours upgrading a pod with a smaller and faster engine—custom designed by me—and wanted to invite her to try it out with me. I thought she'd be excited to be the first one to test it, but now all that is forgotten.

I watch as she smiles up at him, and my surprise turns to hurt and then to anger. How could she moan and writhe in my arms and then smile at this male and let him touch her?

I clench my fists. Doesn't she understand that she is mine? Does she not understand Lokarian claiming?

I stumble back out of the dining hall, crashing into a few Lokarian cadets and mumbling half-hearted apologies. I barrel down the corridor and around a corner, running headlong into a Lokarian in a military uniform.

"Koran?" He grabs my by the shoulders as we both stagger back from the impact.

I force myself to look up. Mikaeus stands in front of me, his face quizzical.

"You okay?" He tilts his head at me. "You look like you're running from a Lokarian boar."

I shake my head. "I am fine. I apologize for not looking where I was going."

He releases my arms but doesn't step aside. "How are things going with your classes? Are you having better luck with the humans?"

I snap my head up, wondering for a moment if he knows about Brooke. But I do not sense cunning from his open expression.

"Some of the humans are better than I had expected," I tell him. This is true in more ways than one. "What about you? How are the humans surviving hand-to-hand?"

He sighs and scrapes a hand through his hair, metal flashing at his wrist from his adornments. "Challenging. The females are very small. I do not see how I will get them to be proficient enough to move on."

"Their size does not mean they are not skilled."

He frowns. "I do not see how being skilled in computer systems will help her in my class."

I do not know what or who he is talking about—I do not think it is Brooke—but he seems genuinely concerned. "Is there one human you have in mind?"

He jerks his head up, seems to realize he's talking to me, then clears his throat. "No. Only a general observation."

I suspect that is not true, but I do not say anything. I have my own problems with the human females. Remembering Brooke makes me glance behind Mikaeus. I do not wish for her to come out of the dining hall and see me, and I cannot bear to see her with *him.*

The Lokarian shakes his head. "You are right. I should not be worrying about something so trivial. Not when there is a Skrum spy in our midst."

I shift from one foot to the other, glad I have destroyed the one thing that could make me appear to have divided loyalties. "Have they made any headway in finding the traitor?"

"Not as far as I know, but I cannot imagine any Lokarian doing such a thing or any human having the access or know how to pull it off."

I know what he means. "Agreed, but if there is a spy, then one of those must be the case."

Mikaeus's frown turns into a scowl. "If there is a spy, Daryx will find him."

I do not know much about the academy head, but I tend to agree with the Lokarian. Daryx seems smart and relentless.

"Between the spy and the missing cadets, he has much to handle," Mikaeus says. "I do not envy him."

"Nor I, although who is to say the cadets will not wander back to campus with hangovers and tales of being lost in the mountains?"

Mikaeus eyes me. "Let us hope. We have never had academy cadets go AWOL." He thumps me on the arm. "I suppose I need to get back to work." He grins. "More cadets to torture."

He strides away from me, and I pivot to head in the opposite direction. I move quickly down the spiraling staircase, out of the building, and across the campus toward the pod track. Only when I know there is no one within earshot, so I take my device out of my pocket and punch in a series of numbers.

"Report," I say when a gruff voice answers.

"We did what you asked."

"I know. I got your transmission. Did you do more than I requested?" My heart races and I close my eyes for a moment, bracing for the news that my Vratvos brothers have taken things too far.

"They were dropped off in the mountains. Nothing more." The voice on the other end lets out a menacing chuckle. "We needed to do nothing more to have them shaking with fear."

"And they cannot recognize you?"

A scornful laugh. "You think we do not know what we are doing? You've been away too long, Koran."

I ignore this thinly veiled insult.

"They will find their way back soon. If not, they are worthless cadets and deserve to die wandering aimlessly on their own planet."

I do not respond to this, wondering for a moment if the Lokarians who attacked Brooke received a fitting punishment. Then I remember seeing the males standing above her and jeering as one pressed her to the ground, grinding himself into her. No, they deserved this. I was more merciful than I should have been.

"Don't worry, Koran," the voice is serious. "They know that if they utter a word about what happened to them, if they do anything to deviate from the story that they got drunk and wandered off, then the next time we will cut their throats while they sleep."

If the Kurvak cadets knew that their captors were Vratvos, they would not doubt the threats in the least.

"I will tell Glatzor you send your best."

The line goes dead, and I exhale loudly. I should not have called on my clan to help, but I could not exact revenge on the cadets without losing my position at the academy. And I could not allow the Kurvaks to get away with hurting the female—my female.

I grind my teeth as I take more long steps to reach the garage. I already owe my clan more than I can ever repay. What is one more debt? But I hate knowing that I will never get out from under their control. I will never be free. Even teaching at the academy cannot last. I will have to return to working for the Vratvos. I am too valuable to them, and I owe them too much. As much as I hate it, I owe my life to my clan, and I know they will not let my debt go uncollected.

My stomach is roiling as I enter the empty garage, grateful I have no more classes for the day. I am in no mood to deal with cadets. Between the potential Skrum spy, exacting revenge on the Kurvak cadets, and seeing Brooke and that human together, my body buzzes as if it's been shot full of electricity. I'm almost vibrating with rage and frustration as I begin to work on one of the broken pods.

The hard, metal tools in my hands and the sharp scent of fuel calm me as I work, the sun falling lower in the sky and sending warm shards of light across the oil-stained floor. There is nothing but the sounds of clanging steel as I go over and over what I saw—Brooke smiling up at him, him wrapping an arm protectively around her as if she was his.

"She is not his," I mutter to myself, attempting to push the image from my mind for the hundredth time.

He is not the one who saved her from the Kurvak. He is not the one who risked everything to punish those who hurt her. He is not the first male to claim her. She is not his.

I lean my forehead against the cool body of the pod and breathe in to steady my hammering heart. No matter how much I try to calm myself, I cannot douse my jealous rage, but I know I cannot send my Vratvos brothers after yet another cadet. Especially not a human one.

CHAPTER TWENTY-TWO

Brooke

I flop back on my bed, glad I didn't have a tough afternoon. I'd much rather learn how to fire a Lokarian sniper rifle than go more rounds on the grappling mats, although what I'd really like to be doing is burning off my stress with a few laps on the pod track.

I drape an arm over my forehead and close my eyes, trying to put that idea out of my head. After what Carter told me, I know I should steer clear of the pod track and the instructor. If he's right, Koran is involved with something he shouldn't be.

Even though I have no reason not to believe Carter, I also can't believe that Koran would be the traitor. He might come off a little dark and dangerous, but that's still a far cry from betraying his people and colluding with the enemy.

Just because you lost your virginity to the guy, doesn't mean he can't be guilty, I remind myself. Every part of me wants the Lokarian to be a misunderstood good guy. Otherwise, I'd have to admit that after waiting twenty-three years, I screwed the one guy who turned out to be a Skrum spy.

I groan out loud. "Way to pick 'em, Brooke."

Despite instinctively trusting Carter, I don't want to assume the worst. There must be legitimate reasons that Koran would be communicating with someone about targets. That's a possibility.

"A really slim one," I mutter to myself.

What are the chances that Koran is exchanging messages with someone about targets at the same time a mole is sending intel to the Skrum, and strange malfunctions are taking place all over campus?

Tears prick the backs of my eyelids as I think about the tall, dark alien with the intense gaze. If he really was a traitor, he'd completely fooled me. I never would have guessed that the Lokarian who saved me from being attacked and was so tender to me when I'd been hurt would be capable of such deceit. Has any of it been real, or has he been playing me the whole time?

I draw in a long breath as I rehash it all in my head. I've known plenty of guys who play fast and loose with the truth, but Koran has never struck me as that type. He actually struck me as the opposite—someone who's willing to do what's right over what's easy or popular.

But if he's such a standup guy, why was he destroying that device? I got a quick look at the small metal device before he'd completely crushed it in his workshop. I don't know what it was, but it's clear he didn't want anyone to get their hands on it.

My stomach tightens as I think about what I've seen, and what Carter has seen. I told him we should keep it to ourselves for now, but that was only because I didn't want to believe Koran was guilty. The more I think about it, though, the more I think we should tell someone before it's too late.

I huff out an exasperated breath. "What a fucking mess."

"Brooke?" Autumn pokes her head into my open door.

I sit up, blinking rapidly. "Hey. I didn't know you were back."

She jerks a thumb toward the central living area. "Wait until you hear what Layla heard in explosives class."

I jump up and follow Autumn out to where the other two women are lounging on the sleek furniture. Layla's blonde hair hangs behind her as she leans her head back on the couch, and Elena has her long legs tucked under her on one of the chairs.

"So, what's up?" I ask, my pulse fluttering in anticipation. "Autumn says you heard some news. Is it about the mole?"

I cross to the other end of the couch and sit. If she tells me they apprehended Koran, I do not want to be standing when I hear. I've never fainted, but there's always first time.

Layla straightens, dragging a hand through her hair. "Nope. Even better. You know those asshole Lokarian cadets who walk around like they own the place?"

That definitely didn't narrow it down since most of the Lokarian cadets seemed pretty cocky to me.

"You're going to have to be more specific," Autumn says, taking the words out of my mouth.

Layla pulled her legs onto the couch and crisscrossed them in front of her. "Three of them who wear jewelry." Her eyes lingered on Autumn. "The ones that gave you a hard time the first day in the dining hall."

Autumn's expression hardens. "*Those* Lokarians?"

Layla nods and the two exchange a look.

"What happened in the dining hall?" Elena asks, her spine stiffening.

"It's nothing." Autumn gives a wave of her hand. "They were being dicks, but Layla told them off for me."

Layla grins. "Trust me. It was my pleasure."

My gut churns. Unless I'm mistaken, it sounds like the Lokarian cadets who harassed Autumn are the same ones who attacked me. I taste bitterness in the back of my throat, as I remembering hot breath on my neck as one of them pressed his heavy body against me.

"I wish I'd been there." Elena's gray eyes are stormy.

"Anyway." Layla leans her elbow on her knees. "These guys apparently were AWOL for the past day or so."

"What?" My voice cracks. "They're gone?"

"*Were* gone," Layla corrects. "From what I heard some Lokarians saying in my last class, they reappeared about an hour ago, totally dehydrated and mumbling about getting drunk and wandering off."

"Seriously?" Autumn shakes her head. "I thought these guys were supposed to be super-disciplined."

Layla shrugs. "Maybe they were blowing off some steam, but I know that they are in deep shit. For Lokarians, going AWOL is a big deal. If they hadn't turned up voluntarily, they could have been executed. Even now, they may be kicked out."

I can't speak. I know these are the cadets who assaulted me, and I know Koran had something to with this. He'd promised to make them pay more than he had when he'd pulled them off me and roughed them up, but I hadn't given it much thought. To be honest, I'd been way too wrapped up in the excitement of our illicit relationship and the mind-blowing sex. But I also realize that these cadets could have been the targets in the transmission, which would mean Koran isn't a traitor.

"You okay, girl?" Autumn asks, and everyone glances over at me.

Elena's eyebrows arch. "You are pretty pale."

"I'm just surprised by the story, that's all." I attempt to make my voice artificially bright. "It's pretty crazy that cadets would disappear and then turn back up like that."

"I hope they kick them out." Autumn sits on one arm of the couch. "They're bullies."

She doesn't know the half of it, I think, although it sounds like she got a little taste of their charm.

"Is there any chance they're the spies?" Autumn asks.

Layla steeples her fingers together. "That's a really good question."

Elena slides her feet to the floor and leans forward. "Pretending to be drunk and lost would be a good cover, if you needed to make a drop."

We all study Elena, and I wonder if the others are also curious about the specialized skills she doesn't talk about.

I know that the reason the cadets went missing almost certainly had to do with Koran and not being traitors, but I also can't say that. Then I'd have to admit the attack, that the pod instructor had saved me, and what had happened next. And I'm not ready to do that yet, as much as I like the suite mates who have become my friends.

I think about Koran and what he's done for me, and my heart beats faster. I've never had someone do something like this for me. It both thrills me and terrifies me, which pretty much sums up my feelings about the sexy Lokarian.

"You know what?" I stand quickly. "I just remembered something I have to do."

Layla narrows her gaze at me. "Now?"

"I told Carter I'd study with him," I lie. "We have a flight test tomorrow."

Autumn smiles knowingly. "Have fun."

I feel bad lying to her and making her think I'm into Carter, but I'm not ready to tell her that I'm falling hard for a Lokarian instructor who either exacted revenge on a bunch of cadets or might be a spy for the Skrum.

CHAPTER TWENTY-THREE

Koran

I know when the cadets wander back onto campus. Even on the outskirts of the campus, there are hushed conversations and snippets of gossip that make their way through the doors of the garage. The academy is practically humming with the news, but I do not venture outside, even as night falls and the air turns cool and crisp.

I know I should be worried. The cadets certainly suspect who was behind their abduction and subsequent dumping in the mountains, even if they can't prove anything. But I know that to admit their suspicions they would need to admit my motives, which would mean admitting to accosting a fellow cadet. A human female cadet. The price for that would certainly be expulsion.

No, the more I think about it, the more I am sure the cowards will keep their mouths shut and take whatever punishment is meted out. They should be grateful that my

Vratvos brothers didn't kill them, and I'm sure they know this, as well.

Now that I am no longer worried about the missing cadets, my mind is free to focus on the female. As much as I want to forget about seeing her with the human, I cannot.

I think back to him speaking to me about her. Why hadn't I seen it then? Was he putting in a good word for her not because she was his friend, as he claimed, but because they are involved? The idea makes my blood boil, and I twist my wrench too hard, snapping a chain on the pod I'm repairing.

"*Vlak*." I slam down the tool, the metal clattering to the floor. How have I let this female get under my skin? I cannot work. I can barely think. She consumes my thoughts.

I am glad I am far away from my clan. They would never let me live down an obsession such as this. Vratvos do not let themselves be ruled by females.

But they have never seen a human female like Brooke, I think, my cock hardening at the thought of her small, lithe body and contrasting soft curves. She is nothing like Lokarian females, and my feelings for her are like nothing I've ever experienced before. I have buried my cock in my share of females, but it was never like this. My need to hold her and protect her and claim her is like a fever I cannot shake.

My breath heaves in my chest. I have been working for half the day and my legs burn from hunching over the pod engine, but the work is the only thing keeping me from storming across the campus and finding the human Carter. I know I cannot confront him, because I will not be able to restrain myself.

The hand on my back makes me instinctively jump up and whirl around, snatching the wrist and twisting it up behind the intruder's back and then forcing their body over the seat of the pod. It is only when I am pressed up against her small frame that I realize it's Brooke.

She lets out a shocked scream, but I wrap an arm around her

and clamp a hand over her mouth, my anger too raw to release her. Not yet.

She wriggles and jerks as she realizes that I'm not letting her go.

I put my head to the side of hers. "I saw you."

She stills and mumbles into my palm, but I am not ready to hear her excuses.

"I saw you with him in the dining hall," I continue. "Smiling and laughing and letting him touch you."

She shakes her head, but I don't release my grasp. Instead, I release her wrist and run my hand down the side of her body, my fingers skimming the side of her breast. "I will not watch another male touch what is mine."

Her protests beneath my hand get louder, and she bucks against me, but my weight keeps her easily pinned down. My cock is a hard bar pressing against her ass, and I savor her body beneath me. "You are mine, and no one else's."

Her breathing is ragged, and her cheeks flushed, but her eyes flash dark and deadly as she twists her head to look at me. I move my hand off her mouth but instantly crush my lips to hers, swallowing her cries. She fights me for a moment before moaning as her tongue swirls with mine. I drag a hand down her throat, dipping it down her shirt and cupping one breast. I squeeze gently, then rub my thumb over the pebbled flesh of her nipple. Her moans become deeper, and she arches into me.

When I finally pull away, she gasps for breath.

"Get off me. You're being crazy and jealous, and he's just a friend."

I do not let her go, my thumb still circling her nipple. "Friends do not touch like that."

"On Earth they do."

I pause at this. I do not know how males and females interact on her planet. But I do know how they act on mine.

"On Lokar, only a male who has fucked you would touch you like that."

She lets out a breath that's half a laugh. "He hasn't fucked me. I promise." She glares at me. "I'm not like that. You think I'm going to lose my virginity to you and then go out and sleep with someone else the next day?"

Some of the fight drains out of me as I see that her eyes glisten. I lean my head into her neck, inhaling the scent of her. "You are mine. I cannot bear to see another male touch you."

"I'm getting that. Is that why you had those Lokarian cadets dumped out in the mountains?"

I still, knowing I do not want to lie to her. "I told you I would punish them."

"You need to be careful," she whispers. "Carter already thinks you're up to something. That's what he was telling me."

My upper lip curls at the mention of the human. "Carter knows nothing."

"And you should hope no one knows what you did, although I can't say I'm not happy those assholes suffered."

I pull her closer, pleased that she knows I got her some measure of justice.

"But you need to chill out after this, okay?" she says. "You can't fight my battles for me, and you sure as hell can't run around beating up any guy who talks to me. Just because I'm friends with someone from home doesn't mean I'm fucking them." Her voice lowers as her eyes flare. "I don't want anyone but you."

My cock aches at her words and at the dark invitation in her gaze. "You are the only female I want." I do not tell her it is more than want. I need her.

"So, are you?" She purrs, swiveling her ass against my cock.

I tilt my head at her. "Am I?"

"Going to fuck me, Koran?" She gives me a wicked smile. "I've been waiting all day, you know."

With a growl, I jerk her pants down and angle her hips up, biting my lip as I see how wet she is for me. I tug my own pants down and fist my cock in one hand, notching it between her slick folds. "This," I say, as I thrust myself hard inside her, "is mine."

CHAPTER TWENTY-FOUR

Brooke

I tiptoe down the corridor, holding my boots so my feet don't make noise on the stone floors. I've managed to make it all the way across the campus and back into the dorm without being spotted, but only because I'm small and move quickly.

I have got to stop doing this, I think to myself. It's only a matter of time before I get caught and have some serious explaining to do. Not that I know what I could possibly say to justify sneaking around way after curfew so the pod instructor can bend me over a pod and fuck me senseless.

Just thinking about his cock inside me sends a twinge between my legs, and I know I'll be sore in the morning.

I give my head a small shake as if dislodging the fog that seems to settle over me when I'm with Koran. I went down to the pod track to confront him, and I ended up screaming his name as he hammered into me again and again.

I flash back to him gripping my bare hips as he pounded into me, my hands splayed across the pod seat as I moaned. Then he'd flipped me around and laid me across the pod with my knees hooked over his shoulders. I bite my bottom lip to keep from groaning as I think of his face, sweaty and wild as he'd stroked into me again and again. You couldn't blame a girl for getting distracted by that, especially once I knew he wasn't a traitor.

Pressing my palm to the panel outside my suite, the lock clicks, and I nudge the door open with my shoulder. The central living area is dark, and I can barely make out the shapes of furniture as I grope my way across toward my bedroom. The four bedroom doors that circle the living area are closed, so I fumble to open my door, hoping that no one hears me.

I pause after stepping inside my room, placing my boots on the floor and letting out a breath. I'm so relieved to have made it back without getting busted I promise myself I will never, ever do it again.

It's too late to bother changing, and I don't want to make any more noise, so I grope my way to the bed and pull back the covers, slipping underneath and rolling over.

"What the heck?"

Shit! I roll off the bed and onto the floor. "Autumn?" My voice is a hiss in the darkness.

"Brooke?" Autumn's hysterical tone has calmed. "What's going on?"

"You tell me." I pick myself up and stand, rubbing my sore ass. "Why are you in my room?"

"Your room?" She clicks on the light next to the bed and the room is illuminated by a warm glow from several wall sconces.

I glance around and quickly see that I am, in fact, in Autumn's bedroom. "Fuck me. Your door is right next to mine. I must have opened the wrong one in the dark."

She angles her head, assessing me. "You want to tell me

exactly what kind of studying leaves your hair looking like that?"

I put a hand to my tousled hair, remembering Koran tangling his hand in it and using it to pull my head back for a hard kiss.

"And why your cheeks just turned red?" She swings her feet over the side of the bed and folds her arms over her chest. "What's really going on with you and Carter?"

I hesitate for a second, considering lying to her and telling her that I'm involved with Carter. But that wouldn't be fair to Carter, and I don't want to keep any more secrets from Autumn. I may have only known her a little over a week, but our mutual suffering during hand-to-hand combat class has definitely made us closer.

"I wasn't with Carter."

Her eyebrows pop up. "You don't have to say that to protect him. I'm not going to tell on you two."

I shake my head, dropping my eyes. "I was with someone, just not him."

She's quiet, and the silence yawns between us.

"It's Koran." The words tumble out of me. "I'm involved with Koran. I know it's wrong, and I could probably get expelled for it and he could definitely get removed, but I can't help it. I don't know what it is about the guy, but I can't stay away from him. It's like I'm under some sort of spell."

She stares at me for a second. "Koran?"

"The pod instructor."

Then her eyes really go wide. "You're doing one of the Lokarian instructors?"

"Shh!" I motion with my hands for her to lower her voice. "I know, I know. It's bad, isn't it?"

She makes a face. "I don't know. I didn't exactly read up on the rules for sleeping with the alien instructors, because it never occurred to me that would be a thing."

"Obviously that was before we saw them."

She shoots me a look, but the corners of her mouth quiver into a grin. "I'll admit that your pod guy is hot, but I thought you hated him. Isn't he the one who kicked you out of class and wouldn't let you ride and made you come late to clean his...?" She slaps a hand over her mouth. "Is that what you've been doing when you were supposed to be cleaning pods?"

My cheeks warm. "No. Not at first."

She gives me a look like she doesn't believe me.

I hold up one palm. "I swear. Nothing happened—nothing serious at least—until he stopped the Lokarian cadets who were attacking me and carried me back to the garage."

Autumn's mouth gapes open. "I beg your pardon? What Lokarian cadets? What attack? Is that why your palms got all scraped up?" Her brows furrow with concern. "Are you okay? They didn't...?"

I shake my head, guilt that I've kept all of this from my friend like a stab to my gut. I can see from the expression on her face that she's both shocked and hurt. "Koran stepped in before they could do much more than push me down and scare me. I didn't tell you because I didn't want anyone to know that it was Koran who beat the crap out of the guys."

Autumn nibbles on the corner of her lower lip. "Wait a second. Are these the same Lokarian cadets who vanished and then turned back up with a lame excuse about getting drunk and wandering off?"

"I don't know for sure that Koran was involved with that, but I'm pretty sure he was. He told me that he would make them pay for hurting me."

"I'm liking this Koran guy more and more."

I smile, warmth spreading in my chest as I think about him and how gingerly he carried me and tended to my cuts. "He's not as scary as he looks."

"So, Koran saved you from those jerk cadets and then you two…?"

I nod. "I've been sneaking out to see him."

"Wow. You did a good job of hiding it. I was convinced you and Carter had something going."

"You aren't the only one. Koran was convinced that I'm more than friends with Carter."

"You're lucky he didn't try to beat him up, too," Autumn says. "I get the idea that these Lokarians are used to settling things with their fists."

"He would have, if I hadn't convinced him that I'm not into Carter."

Autumn gives me a wicked smile. "Wonder how you did that?"

I ignore her pointed look. "The problem is, Carter is convinced that Koran is hiding something, and that he might be the Skrum mole."

Autumn flips her long brown hair off her shoulder. "Why would he think that?"

I shrug. "He's Naval intelligence and was trained to read Lokarian before we came here. He apparently read a transmission that Koran received, and it said something about targets."

All levity fades from Autumn's face. "That doesn't sound good, Brooke. Are you sure Koran isn't involved in something? I mean, I know you're really into the guy, but how much do you know about him?"

"I know he's a good guy and that he's not the spy. You'll have to trust me on this."

"I will, but you're going to need more than that if Carter tells someone about what he saw." She waves a hand toward the window. "The entire academy is looking for the spy."

"I know, I know." I pace a small circle in front of her. "I went down to the pod track tonight to warn him."

She gives me a withering look. "That obviously went well.

Do you need me to go with you next time, so you can keep your pants on?"

"No." I hate the implication that I'm so sex-crazed that I can't control myself although it's a little bit true. Okay, a lot true. "I'll talk to him today."

She's right. I do need to persuade Koran to talk to Carter before things get out of hand. Carter won't keep it to himself, if he believes Koran is a traitor.

"As long as you promise to talk to him, I promise not to breathe a word of this to anyone." Autumn winks at me and crosses one knee over the other. "Now, since you woke me up in the dead of night, you'd might as well tell me what these hot aliens are like in bed." Her eyes flick to my hair again. "Or out of it."

CHAPTER TWENTY-FIVE

Koran

I walk briskly toward the main academy building, glancing up at the massive metal arch extending out over the entrance. Sunlight glints off the shiny surface, making me shield my eyes. I should be tired, since Brooke was with me until the early hours of the morning, but instead I feel like I could leap up the obsidian mountains in a few bounds.

Knowing that she is mine and mine alone makes my heart beat faster. I cannot explain how touching her makes me complete, but when I am buried inside her, all my doubts and fears vanish, and I am invincible. I think of seeing her again tonight, and my fingers tingle as if anticipating the softness of her skin. I mostly stifle a growl that builds in my throat and a pair of human cadets turn in surprise as I pass them on the stone path. I nod and continue walking, trying not to laugh as happiness burbles up inside me.

I am unaccustomed to these feelings. I know the pleasure of

a female's body, but I have never experienced this stirring deep within myself. I have never cared about another's pleasure and happiness more than my own, and I never could have imagined it would be a human who would make me feel these wonderful, unsettling emotions.

Passing through the wide holographic doors, I take the curving stairs two at a time. My boots thump loudly against the hard, polished floors, but they are only two of many, as cadets in both blue and black uniforms hurry down the corridors.

I make my way to the room at the end of a long hall. I have been here before, but only to meet with the academy head alone. When I enter the long conference room with glass walls overlooking the sharp, black, mountain range, I recognize many other instructors already in clear chairs around the frosted-glass, oval table.

I spot Mikaeus and an empty chair next to him and sink gratefully into it.

He arches a brow at me. "Someone is already having a good day."

I attempt to make my face expressionless as I shrug. "No better or worse than any other."

He nods, but eyes me suspiciously as the academy head enters the room and strides down the wall of windows to the far end.

The gold Lokarian crest on Daryx's uniform glints like the strands of silver in his hair as he pivots to face us, thumping his right fist on his left shoulder. The other military officers respond to his salute in kind. "Thank you all for coming before your classes begin. I wanted to update you on several matters."

I lean forward and rest my elbows on the table, all earlier giddiness banished from my mind. There is a sharp wrinkle between the elder Lokarian's eyes, and it is clear from the dark circles underneath that he hasn't slept well of late.

"Is this about the AWOL cadets?" one of the other instructors asks.

Daryx shakes his head. "No. Those cadets have been dealt with appropriately."

I refrain from letting out a sigh of relief. Involving my clan to punish the cadets who hurt Brooke was not a wise move, and I am grateful that I am not currently answering for it.

"This is about the treachery within our ranks," Daryx continues.

Low murmuring passes from one end of the table to the other and dark looks are exchanged.

"Does this also have to do with the malfunctions throughout the academy?" an instructor with braids asks.

"More than likely the saboteur is connected to the traitor, or they are one and the same," Daryx says. "I suspect the malfunctions have been meant to distract us."

"Then they have worked." Another teacher leans his elbows on the table. "The temperature in the archery studio dropped so low overnight, all my bow strings froze and snapped."

I've heard about these odd power fluctuations and system glitches, but my pod track is so old school it has little that would be affected by the centralized system.

"In addition to the malfunctions, we have been able to determine that critical information has been copied from our encrypted virtual storage." The academy head rocks back on his heels, the braid down the side of his head swinging.

"A hack?" Mikaeus's face is pinched.

Daryx scowls. "No. The individual who accessed the information had the proper codes."

I look down at my hands, my relief growing. Not only were the ship cockpits and pod schematics I'd photographed not classified, they were not hidden behind encryption. My information gathering seems almost amateurish, compared to what the academy head is describing. It is also something that no Vratvos could pull off. Not unless we were given access codes, and only members of the Lokarian Senate have those. As subversive as my clan could be, we had yet to turn a member of the Lokarian leadership. At least, not that I knew of.

"Are you saying…?"

I turn to see a Lokarian with a silver medallion peeking from underneath his black uniform.

"Yes, Zarryn," the academy head answers. "Only a member of the Lokarian Senate could have shared the codes used to access our information."

Instead of dark muttering, the room is silent as the reality of this settles on all of us.

"A member of the Lokarian leadership is compromised?" Mikaeus asks, breaking the silence. "How is this possible?"

Daryx lets out a weary breath. "We do not know this for sure. There are many ways the codes could have gotten into the wrong hands. The member of the Senate might not even be aware."

More glances are exchanged, and I know everyone is thinking what I am. It is unlikely that a member of the Lokarian leadership was compromised without his or her knowledge. Even if they were, who at the academy would have been able to do it? I have never even laid eyes on a member of our highest ruling body.

"Is there a way we can determine which member of the Senate is behind the breach?" Zarryn asks.

Daryx gives a curt shake of his head. "The codes are not individual."

"Then can we find out who on the campus used them, and where?" Zarryn's voice rises. "There must be a way to track down the thief."

"We have our best on it."

Mikaeus clears his throat. "We should use the humans."

All heads swivel to him, including my own.

He lifts his eyes and straightens his shoulders. "Earth sent us some of their best hackers. It would be foolish to embark on this joint mission and not use what they know."

I wonder how he knows about the hackers since his specialty is hand-to-hand combat, but I don't ask.

Daryx stares at him for a moment, then nods. "You are correct. We should not discount the humans."

I can tell not everyone agrees, but Mikaeus seems pleased by the response, leaning back in his chair and crossing his arms over his chest.

"If the information has already been taken, should we assume the Skrum have it?" A Lokarian I recognize as the flight instructor leans against a wall with his legs crossed at the ankles. "I would like to know if I should be putting our ships on standby."

"So far, there have been no transmissions off-world, Captain," Daryx says. "We suspect that the thief downloaded the information with plans to send it later."

Zarryn scrapes a hand through his hair. "So, it's a race to find the traitor before they can get the information to the Skrum?"

"Do we know what the Skrum want so badly?" I ask. There are many things that our enemy could want—security codes to our shields, information about the size of our fleet, details about the human military.

Daryx braces both hands against the edge of the conference table and levels his gaze at us. "They want the plans for this academy."

CHAPTER TWENTY-SIX

Brooke

"What are you doing here?" Carter asks when he sees me waiting for him outside the men's dorm.

It's still early in the morning, and part of me is shocked I actually got up and out so early. Then again, I've been wired since I got home and confided in Autumn. Talking to her made me feel so much better, I convinced myself I needed to talk to Carter and tell him what I know. I only slept a couple of hours before getting up and showering, and the hair I pulled up into a ponytail is still damp

"Looking for you."

As usual, the Naval intelligence officer's dark-blue uniform is starched, and his short hair is neatly combed. "I didn't know you were a morning person."

"I'm not, but I needed to talk to you before class."

His teasing expression becomes serious. "Is everything okay?"

"I'm fine." I motion to a stone ledge outside the dorm where we can sit. "But it's about that thing we were talking about yesterday."

"The pod instructor?" He glances around, even though there is no one else near us.

I bob my head up and down. "I know you think he's dirty, but I don't think he is."

"Okay." Carter looks at me, and I can see that he's genuinely curious. "Explain."

I draw in a breath. "The transmission you saw didn't have anything to do with him acquiring secrets for the Skrum. The targets it referenced were the Lokarian cadets who went AWOL."

Now he looks really confused. "That doesn't make any sense. Why would the academy pod instructor have anything to do with cadets wandering away from campus?"

"Because they didn't wander away, and I'm pretty sure they're just too scared to admit it."

He cocks his head at me. "You're not making a lot of sense."

"I know, I know." I wring my hands, hesitant to admit the next part, but knowing I have to. "It makes sense if you understand why it was those particular cadets who disappeared."

"You mean because they're assholes who think that their fancy clan makes them better than everyone else?"

I can't help grinning. "So, you *do* know them."

"They like to show off in the advanced pod class, but I usually ignore them. And the instructor doesn't mind knocking them down a peg or two when he needs to. Are you saying he had it out for them because they were dicks in class?"

I shake my head, not meeting his eyes. "It's because they were dicks to me. More than that, actually."

He's quiet as I take another breath and continue. "Remember that night I was going to talk to Kor—the instructor? Well, I got a later start, like I told you. What I didn't tell you was that those three Lokarians were waiting for me. I guess they'd heard us talking in flight class."

"Shit. I forgot they were in that class with us." He lowers his voice. "Brooke, what happened?"

"Basically, they got the jump on me. I guess they were still pissed that I'd shown them up that first day on the pod track. Apparently, Lokarian egos are smaller than Lokarian..." I glance up, my face warm. "Sorry. So, yeah, it was dark and no one else was outside after hours. They pushed me down and jumped on me. I don't know what they would have done if Koran hadn't appeared and beaten the crap out of them."

I look up and see that Carter's face is fierce. "I can't believe those assholes did that to you. We should report them and get their sorry asses expelled."

"That's the thing. Koran said he was going to make sure they paid for what they'd done. He's responsible for them disappearing and wandering back to campus shell-shocked and too freaked out to talk about it."

"But he hasn't left campus. I've had class with him, and I've heard the other cadets talking. He hasn't missed any of their classes."

I nibble my bottom lip. "I know. I think the transmission you saw means that he had someone else snatch the guys for him."

"Who could do that?" Carter looks around us. "I know the campus doesn't have walls, but I think it would be tough to kidnap people without being seen."

I shrug. "Maybe not. Koran is a member of the Vratvos clan. I read up on them. They're like the mob and a biker gang all wrapped up in one."

"That explains why he doesn't wear a uniform like the other instructors." He shakes his head. "You really think he would have asked a bunch of his criminal buddies to kidnap these cadets and dump them in the middle of nowhere? That seems pretty extreme, even for overly aggressive Lokarians. Especially since it would be risking his position as instructor."

"I know." I wait until a human cadet walks out of the dorm and is far enough away that he can't hear us. "But he's pretty overprotective and possessive."

"Overprotective and possessive?" Carter frowns. "Why would he be...?" His mouth falls open. "Brooke, you're not telling me that you're...? You and the Lokarian pod guy aren't...?"

"Yep."

He continues to gape at me.

"You can close your mouth now." My cheeks burn under his gaze. "It's not so crazy that he could be attracted to me, is it?"

Carter clamps his mouth shut. "That he would be attracted to you? Of course, that's not crazy. Any guy would be attracted to you. What's crazy is a smart woman like you falling for one of our academy instructors. Not to mention, an instructor who might or might not have arranged an abduction of some of our fellow cadets."

"Cadets who deserved it," I remind him, holding up a finger.

He narrows his eyes at me. "I won't argue with that, but I will argue that we don't know for sure what that message I saw meant. The only thing we know is that some weird things are going on around here, and your guy seems to be wrapped up in at least some of them."

"I know he's not a traitor. You have to believe me."

His stern expression softens. "Of anyone on this entire planet, I trust you the most. That doesn't mean I trust Koran, but it does mean I'll give him the benefit of the doubt. For you."

"I knew I could count on you." I throw my arms around him and give him a big hug, then pull back, afraid I've gone too far.

Carter just laughs. "I'll say one thing for you. You've made my first week here anything but dull."

"Texas girls don't do boring."

"Obviously." He stands. "So, are we going to go talk to your boy or what?"

"Now?"

"Actually, I need to get me some coffee first. Or what the Lokarians call coffee. Then I suggest we go down to the pod track and get some answers."

I fall in step with Carter as he heads toward the main building and the dining hall. "Don't be surprised if he isn't too thrilled to see me with you."

His lips quirk up as he glances over at me. "And why is that?"

"He might have thought we were more than friends, but I straightened him out right away."

"I guess I should be glad the guy didn't dump me in the middle of nowhere," Carter says under his breath.

I remember Koran's blazing eyes when he'd accused me of sleeping with Carter. "You have no idea."

CHAPTER TWENTY-SEVEN

Brooke

It doesn't take long for us to get the Lokarian equivalent of coffee from the dining hall, but I'm still impatient as we wind down the stone path toward the pod track.

"You'd think a planet this advanced could master a mocha," Carter grumbles, taking a swig from his cup and grimacing.

"Subtle flavors don't seem to be their thing." Most of the Lokarian food we've had is spicy, and their take on coffee is sharp and bitter. I gave up drinking it after the first day, opting to be a little sleepy the first hours of the morning instead of choking down the thick beverage.

Carter swallows and cringes. "At least it wakes me up."

"I think that's only because it tastes so bad."

He grins at me. "You might be right."

Even though his legs are long, he's modulated his strides to match my shorter ones. I'm used to practically running to keep up with people, especially men, so I appreciate the gesture.

"I have a question." I take my eyes off the glass-domed pod garage in the distance and glance quickly at him.

"You mean in addition to the list of questions we have for Koran? Fire away."

"You said earlier that any guy would be attracted to me, right?"

He nods, his eyes narrowing and one eyebrow quirking up as he looks over at me.

"But you've always been fine with us just being friends, right? I mean, you've never tried to be more. Not that I'm asking you to, but I thought it was because you didn't think I was pretty, but if you think any guy would be attracted to me—"

"Are you asking me to hit on you, Butler?"

I shake my head hard. "No, it's just…"

"I'd have to blind to think you aren't attractive." He winks at me. "But you're not my type, babe."

"Oh." Relief washes over me, although I don't know why. Carter not being attracted to me is one less thing to worry about, and I like having a male friend I don't need to watch myself around. He reminds me of my brothers even more now. Without being given a noogie every two minutes, that is, which makes him even better than my brothers.

He angles his head at me. "Are we cool?"

"Totally." We slow our pace as we reach the doors of the pod garage. Even though I know he doesn't have a morning class today, the double doors are pulled open. That means Koran is here, which doesn't surprise me in the least. If I hadn't seen his quarters, I might believe he sleeps with his pods.

Carter puts a hand on my arm to hold me back before I walk inside. I pause, thinking he wants to discuss our strategy, or who should talk first, but he puts a finger to his lips.

Before I can ask him why he wants to sneak inside, I hear it. Deep voices. My pulse flutters as I recognize Koran's deep rumble, but then my breath catches in my throat when I recognize the other sounds. Voices I would know anywhere. Voices I heard laughing as they stood over me. A voice I heard whispering menacingly in my ear as he pressed me into the ground.

I take a step back without thinking about it, and Carter reaches for my hand, holding it tightly in his. The solid warmth of his grip steadies me, and I meet his gaze, his blue eyes calming me.

He puts another finger to his lips, and I nod. The Lokarian cadets should not be here, and it's clear from the tenor of their voices that they aren't making a social call.

I steady my breathing, holding Carter's hand tightly as we slip inside as quietly as possible. We both walk on our toes, ducking behind the closest pod and crouching down.

"I don't know what you're talking about, Vex." Koran's voice is remarkably unconcerned.

The three cadets face him in a semi-circle with their backs to us, and it's clear they have weapons drawn, although I can't see what kind.

Vex, the one who'd straddled me and forced me to the ground, laughs. "You think we don't know who took us? It could only have been a bunch of dirty Vratvos."

"So, you say," Koran's voice is steady. "Did you see them? My clan is distinctive."

"They made sure we didn't see anything," one of the other cadets says. "And they didn't speak."

"Yet you're sure it was the Vratvos?" Now Koran laughs. "I don't think I've ever heard of my clan being silent."

Vex stomps a heavy foot on the floor. "It was them. Who else would have a reason except for you? But you couldn't do it yourself. You have to keep up your sham as an academy instructor, when we all know you're a criminal at heart, just like everyone in your clan."

"It's because of that human, isn't it?" One of the cadets spits out, the disdain clear in his voice. "You were mad we tried to take a taste before you."

Carter tenses next to me.

"No self-respecting Lokarian takes a human's side over one of us," Vex says.

"No Lokarian worth anything attacks a female," Koran growls.

"Do you know who I am?" Vex's voice ricochets off the domed ceiling and fills the cavernous space.

I peek over the top of the pod seat and see Koran with his arms folded across his chest. "A Kurvak who needs to be expelled?"

"My father is on the Senate." Vex waves his weapon as he speaks. "All I have to do is snap my fingers and you'll be sent back to the hole you crawled out of, as will that pretty little human." He chuckles low. "Of course, I may need to fuck her before she's sent back to Earth in disgrace." He sweeps an arm toward his friends. "We all will."

I want nothing more than to jump up and tell them that I'd rather die first, but Carter tightens his grip on my hand.

Koran emits a dark rumbly sound, baring his teeth.

Vex cock his head. "If I didn't know better, I'd say you've already had her. But would she really be stupid enough to fall for a traitor?"

"I'm no traitor," Koran says. "And you know it."

"If anyone on this campus would be a traitor, it would be a Vratvos. Right, brothers?"

His friends nod and laugh.

"But you're the one with a Senator father." Koran's murderous gaze does not waver. "And the codes used to access classified data were only available to members of the Lokarian leadership. Something a Vratvos could never have."

"I'm always surprised when a Vratvos isn't as stupid as he

looks." Vex's words cause his friends to laugh louder. "Very good, pod master. You figured it out before anyone else. Not that it's going to help you."

"So, what's your plan?" Koran asks. "Kill me, plant evidence, and claim you uncovered the traitor and then had to kill me in self-defense?"

Vex shrugs. "Something like that. After all, it will be our word against yours."

One of the other cadets leans forward. "And you'll be dead."

"So why tell me?" Koran puts his hands on his hips and squares his shoulders. "Why not just come in here and shoot me?"

Watching how calm Koran appears, I want to shake him. Why is he provoking these assholes?

"I wanted you to know that you didn't get the better of us." Vex's voice vibrates with fury. "You needed to know that you didn't win. We did."

I turn to Carter, whose expression is thunderous. We've just heard these Lokarian cadets practically admit to treason, but there's no time to go for help. Koran will be dead before anyone could get here.

I motion my head to the pod we're hiding behind, and his eyes widen. I don't have a fully-formed plan, but I know we need to stop these assholes from killing Koran and framing him for treason.

"Ready to test out your skills?" I whisper.

He tilts his head at me. "Please tell me you're not talking about what I think you're talking about."

I cut my eyes to the pod and grin.

Closing his eyes for a moment, he finally opens them and gives a curt nod.

I give him a thumbs up, then lift two earpieces off a nearby rack, handing one to Carter and hooking the other over my ear.

"That's far enough."

We both freeze and look up at the Lokarian cadet standing over us with a blaster pointed at my head.

CHAPTER TWENTY-EIGHT

Koran

I want to both shake Brooke and pull her close to me when I see the cadet walk her and Carter out from behind some pods. For a brief moment, I wonder why she's with the human male, but I force myself not to be jealous. Not when I'm going to need Carter's help to keep Brooke from being killed.

"I would ask what she's doing here." Vex grins at me. "But I think we all know the answer to that question."

Brooke's chin juts out as she walks with her hands up. If she's scared, she isn't letting on.

"So, what's your master plan?" A muscle ticks in Carter's jaw as he walks. "You do know other cadets are going to start showing up for classes soon, right? Or did you not think things through when you decided to take out your fall guy in the middle of the day?"

"Actually, we have you two to thank for our timing." Vex waves Carter toward me with his blaster. "If we hadn't overhead you talking outside the dorm, we wouldn't have needed to move things up."

Brooke shoots me a quick, apologetic look.

"You'll be happy to know that the female had put two and two together, but was convinced you were innocent." Vex steps closer to her and runs his eyes down her body. "I'm glad you showed up when you did. One more loose end that I don't have to worry about tying up later."

Brooke's jaw is clenched, and I see a muscle tick as she glares up at the cadet. It takes all my self-control not to lunge at him, but I know I can't take any chances when his blaster is pointed at her head.

It is only now, seeing her in danger, that I realize that what I feel for Brooke is more than desire or lust. I am in love with her. I think I have been since the moment she stole the pod. I want desperately to tell her, but that would only put her in more danger.

"The human is right, Vex," one of the other cadets says, his gaze flitting to the doors of the garage. "We need to get this over with, so we can get to class and have alibis."

Vex ignores him, running a finger down Brooke's throat and hovering at the neckline of her shirt. "Our alibis are already taken care of."

Brooke's murderous expression doesn't falter, and my chest swells with pride. My female might be small, but she has nerves of steel.

One of the other Lokarian cadets huffs out a breath. "Why won't you tell us who your other contact is?"

"No one can know," Vex snaps. "It's too important. Besides, if I fail, I need someone who can carry out the plan."

Carter's head snaps up, and I know we're thinking that same thing. They have another co-conspirator?

Vex returns his attention back to Brooke, licking his lips.

"I know you get your rocks off by picking on women smaller

than you," Carter says, "but how about you try your luck against someone your own size?"

Vex swivels his gaze to the human, sizing him up quickly and his face breaking into a wide smile. "Who? You?"

"No," I say. "Me."

Vex's gaze shifts between us, and he sighs, relaxing the arm holding his blaster for a second. It's only a momentary slip, but Brooke springs into action so fast I'm almost too stunned to react.

She spins around and lands a kick to his middle, causing Vex to double over. The other two cadets seem as shocked as I am, and Carter quickly disarms one, getting him into a headlock and squeezing hard enough that the Lokarian's face starts to turn red. I dive for the wrench I'd left on the ground and hurl it at the only standing Lokarian, catching him square in the temple and sending him to the floor.

When I turn, Vex is righting himself and leveling his blaster at me. Suddenly, Brooke is on his back, clawing at his face and causing him to shriek as he spins and attempts to dislodge her. He backs into a pod, and it wobbles between the magnetic braces. Brooke releases her grip on his back and falls over the pod and onto the ground, landing in a crouch.

He shoots at her while she ducks and screams.

Diving at him, I wrestle the blaster out of his hand as he fires it, red beams shooting into the air before it hits the floor and slides underneath a row of pods. Vex twists himself out of my grasp and jumps onto a pod, gunning the engine and accelerating out of the garage.

"No, you don't, you fucker," Brooke yells, engaging the energy helmet over her head and leaping onto a pod.

Before I can tell her to stop, she's flying off after the Lokarian traitor.

"*Vlak*," I shout, scanning the garage and seeing Carter standing over both motionless cadets.

He waves an arm at me. "Go after her. I'll make sure these two don't move."

I grunt an acknowledgement, then hoist myself onto the pod I've been working on upgrading, forgoing a helmet. I engage the engine, and it roars to life between my legs. I don't look back again as I fly forward, the extra boost I've given the engine making me clutch the handlebars until my fingers go white.

I zoom out of the garage and cross the pod track, staying so low to the ground I can see dust kick up behind me. The terrain beyond the academy campus is dry and sparse, with dark rock jutting up from the ground and creating an obstacle course that I maneuver through deftly. Patches of greenery are few and far between, and the black earth is dry and cracked.

I squint as the air rushes in my face, wishing I had something to block it, but also loving the rush of the wind as it whips through my hair. Two flashes of white are ahead of me, one flying straight and one weaving back and forth dangerously, dodging the spiky rock formations.

I know exactly which of the cadets is cutting back and forth, and I clench my fingers tighter around the handlebars. Brooke is clearly trying to get Vex to fall, but her maneuvers are dangerous, especially at her speed. I lean down and accelerate faster, the thrust pushing me back as I power forward.

After a few more moments, I'm almost on them, even as I lose them momentarily behind looming rocks as black and shiny as the obsidian mountains.

Vex is a competent flyer, but he continues to dart glances behind him, clearly nervous that Brooke is so close to his tail. For her part, Brooke keeps flying from side to side, forcing Vex to check over both shoulders and for his pod to wobble as he tries to avoid jutting rocks. Her strategy is clever, but I doubt the Lokarian will fall. I have taught him better than that.

I fly even with Brooke, glancing over and seeing the determined look on her face. She is not going to let this go, and I don't know if I blame her.

She motions for me to flank him on one side, and I do so. When she pulls up on his other side, Vex glances between us.

I see the fear etched on his face. He can't outfly us, and he knows it.

As he bends down to accelerate, Brooke flies up and spins in mid-air, bringing her vehicle directly in front of him. Vex turns hard to go around her but loses control of the pod and it flies forward while he pinwheels into the air without it, coming down hard on the ground.

Brooke's wide smile falters as Vex's pod flies toward her, and she ducks as it barely misses her and crashes into a towering rock behind her. My relief almost instantly vanishes as the pod explodes on contact, the ball of fire engulfing Brooke's pod and her.

CHAPTER TWENTY-NINE

Koran

My heart stops as I watch the ball of fire rise high into the air. The charred hull of the pod crashes to the ground under the flames.

No no no no! I shake my head, refusing to believe what I'm seeing.

It's impossible, I think. I can't have lost her. Not now. Not when I've just found her. Not when I've finally realized how madly in love with her I am.

I stop my pod and lower it to the ground, my hands shaking as I hop off and let it fall to one side.

"Brooke!" I bellow over the roar of the fire. The heat makes me lift a hand to shield my face, but I don't care. I rush forward, peering into the flames that are rising from the pod hull and the debris that has rained down. There is no second pod on the ground. Is she injured? Did she escape?

Without giving myself time to think, I rush into the fire, my arms up over my face.

"Brooke!" I yell again. I can barely see through the acrid smoke that burns my throat as I try not to breathe. There is another pop of an explosion, and over that sound, I hear my name.

My head swims from lack of air as I spin around, the orange flames dancing high around me, looking for the source of the voice. Am I imagining it?

"Koran!"

I turn, and see a small form on the other side of the flames. Staggering through a brief gap in the fire, I reach the other side and fall to my knees as Brooke runs forward, catching me under my arms. She buckles under my weight, then lowers me onto my back. We both land on the hard ground with a thump. I wince from the impact, but I'm glad to be out of the fire.

She slaps her hands at my legs, putting out small fires on my pants, then she slaps my chest. "What were you thinking?"

I cough, trying to take a breath but still inhaling smoke. "I thought you were in the fire."

She shakes her head, but her eyes are damp. "And you had to be a hero?"

"I had to save you."

She swipes at her eyes. "Could we please agree to both stop trying to save each other?"

"Only if you agree to stop taking stupid risks."

Her eyes narrow, then she pats my head and a plume of smoke rises from it. "Fine. But only because you literally set yourself on fire for me." She wrinkles her nose. "Burning hair does not small pretty."

I push myself up onto my elbows. "What about Vex?"

She twists her head, and we both look over to the spot where the Lokarian lies crumpled on the ground, a dark, wet pool forming around his head. "If you ask me, he deserved it."

I agree with her, but my stomach churns as I remember that Vex was the only one who knew the identity of yet another co-conspirator. Not even the other Kurvak cadets—and I'm pretty sure one of those is already dead—know who Vex was working with on the plot to betray his planet.

"Koran." She takes my face in her hands, her voice serious. "I'm sorry I ever doubted you."

I shake my head. "I gave you reason to doubt." I meet her eyes. "I won't do that again."

"You also can't dump people in the middle of nowhere as punishment for being mean to me." Her severe look softens. "Although I really appreciate it, and I'm glad you did it. Especially now that we know what those guys were up to."

Instead of making a promise I have no intention of keeping, I cup her face in my hand. "I am not sorry for that, and anyone who hurts you from now on will have me to deal with."

She scowls at me. "Do you really think I need some guy to fight my battles for me?"

Her eyes flash, and my pulse quickens. She's so beautiful when she's angry. "I think you are mine, and I do not forgive anyone who touches my female."

Brooke rolls her eyes and tries to pull away from me. "I don't know if it's a Lokarian thing or a Koran thing, but I'm not digging the women as property idea."

I hold tight to her, enjoying watching her squirm. "I may not own you, but I have claimed you, and in Lokarian tradition, it is my right to defend you to the death. Like it or not, human."

Her blue eyes glitter. "I should kick you in the balls."

"I do not have these 'balls' your human males do."

Her cheeks redden. "I know. It's too bad."

"You would prefer I had them? It seems impractical to have such delicate things hanging outside the body, especially if you would like to kick them."

She huffs out a breath, then the corners of her mouth

tremble into a smile. "You're impossible. I don't know why I'm so crazy about you."

I pause, my gaze raking across her face. "You're crazy about me?"

"Don't let it go to your head, buddy. I still think you're arrogant and bossy."

"And I think you're impulsive and stubborn, but I still can't help loving you."

She puts her hands on her hips. "Maybe I wouldn't have to be so stubborn if you weren't so… Did you say you love me?"

"Yes, but don't let it go to your head." I jerk her body flush to mine and crushing my mouth to hers. Her initial protest squeal soon fades away, and she sinks into the kiss, wrapping her arms around my neck. She moans softly and parts her lips, our tongues tangling as I entwine my fingers in her hair.

My body tingles as I press her to me, loving her soft curves against my hardness. Everything around us disappears, and even the sounds of the fire seem muffled as I disappear into the feel and taste of her.

Only when a hoverpod engine rumbles behind us do I force myself to pull away, looking up at the tall figure swinging his legs over the side of the pod. He takes in the small inferno, dead body, and our charred clothes, and his eyes widen.

"Should I ask what happened here?"

"Carter! You're okay!" Brooke beams up at him.

He nods, giving a quick glance back toward the campus. "One of the other cadets is dead, and I tied up the survivor. I came to tell you that some of the other instructors are heading this way. The explosion was felt all the way back in the garage."

I stiffen, knowing that I have a lot of explaining to do, and also knowing that Carter heard everything.

"Don't worry," Brooke says, as if reading my mind. "We both heard Vex and his friends confess."

"But I am guilty of exacting revenge on them."

Carter clears his throat. "Brooke told me what those guys did to her and tried to do to her. I'm just glad you were there to help her." His eyes shift to the approaching pods then back to me. "They deserved what they got and more, but I don't think them being dumped in the mountains has any relevance to the plot that you uncovered."

I understand what he's saying but not saying. He's not going to rat me out. I meet his eyes and give him a sharp nod.

"But if you ever hurt my friend—" His gaze goes to Brooke. "—all bets are off."

I wrap my arms tighter around my female, knowing that I will never hurt her. "Understood."

CHAPTER THIRTY

Brooke

"I told you, I'm fine." I sit on a metal platform bed in the academy's hospital wing, my feet dangling below me as a Lokarian medic inspects my bruises and burns.

Like most places in the alien school, the room has high ceilings and glass walls, with plenty of natural light. I'd never known that the place even had a hospital wing, but I now know that it sits on the far end of the campus and has a nice view of the manicured lawns and winding, stone paths that connect all the glass-domes and pointy-spired buildings. It's definitely the fanciest hospital room I've ever been in, but it still has the antiseptic scent that seems to be a hallmark of all hospitals, no matter what planet they're on.

"You're lucky, is what you are," Layla says from across the room where she leans against the wall, her arms and legs crossed.

Autumn stands next to me, her face creased with worry. I

smile, trying to reassure her. "I promise you I've had worse accidents than this one."

"Worse than a pod exploding on top of you?" Autumn asks.

"It wasn't on top of me. It was behind me."

The medic dabbing cleanser on my scraped elbows raises an eyebrow at this, but doesn't say anything.

"We can tell." Elena holds up the tattered clothes I'd been wearing, which had been seared all along the back. "Luckily, the fabric was flame resistant, but it still looks like you were the main course at a barbecue.

"Ha ha." I shake a finger at her. "Don't tease a Texas girl about barbecue."

"I can't believe one of the Lokarian cadets was responsible for stealing the encrypted information." Autumn nibbles on her thumbnail. "And he took his own father's codes. There wasn't a need for a skilled hacker, since the guy just waltzed into the systems."

"I knew he was an asshole." I rub a hand across my forehead. "But I had no idea he was a traitor."

"You never know about people." Elena presses her lips together.

I suspect there's more to Elena's statement than she's willing to talk about, but I let the woman's enigmatic statement slide.

"What I can't believe is that you kept your thing with the smoking-hot pod instructor a secret from us." Layla makes a *tsk*-ing noise in her throat. "What happened to friends sharing juicy gossip?"

"Even when the gossip is about me?" I ask.

Layla grins and winks. "Especially then, girl."

I hold my hands up in surrender. "I'm sorry. It all happened pretty fast. I didn't want him to get in trouble, plus, I didn't want to get kicked out and sent back home."

"What happens now?" Layla asks. "The academy head knows about you two now, right?"

I nod. "We came clean. Luckily, he was so grateful to us for uncovering the spy that he's decided to look the other way. As long as I continue to take my classes privately, so it doesn't disturb the other cadets, and he doesn't show me any favoritism."

"Private classes?" Elena flips her long braid off her shoulder. "Is that what we're calling banging the teacher after hours, now?"

My face warms, as I try to give her my most severe look and the medic attending me half-coughs, half-chokes.

"Elena!" Autumn is also blushing. "I'm sure that's not *all* they do."

"Thanks," I say, not sure if that's a ringing endorsement.

Before my friends can tease me any more, Carter sticks his head inside the room. "You decent, Butler?"

"Come on in." I wave him inside. "The Lokarian hospital gowns are much less revealing than the ones on Earth."

He eyes the voluminous, black fabric covering me. "Probably because they're all twice the size of you."

My friends wave hello, and Autumn blushes even more, which I know is because she used to think I was sleeping with Carter.

"I should be released soon." I give the medic a pointed look as he ducks out of the room. "All I have are scratches. The uniform protected me from the worst of the fire. How's Koran?"

Carter shoves his hands in his pockets. I know he's still adjusting to the rough Lokarian being a good guy, and to me being involved with him. I remind myself that he's adapting quicker than my brothers would have. For once, I'm glad to be light years away from them.

"He's fine. Last I saw, he was heading out to be debriefed."

My heart sinks a little. I'd been hoping to see him after I got patched up, but I guess he had a lot more to talk to the headmaster about.

"Any word on the missing co-conspirator?" I ask.

Carter shakes his head. "The cadet who didn't die has no idea. It appears that Vex was the traitor, and the other two were muscle for all his other bad deeds."

"Doesn't make them any less guilty." Elena curls her fingers into fists by her side.

I've filled my friends in on the attack and Koran saving me, but I omitted the part about him taking revenge on them. If they connected the dots to the fact that the cadets who attacked me were the same ones that went AWOL and then wandered back onto campus, they haven't said anything.

"But Vex hadn't sent the information off-planet, right?" Autumn asks. "I mean, last I heard, they hadn't tracked any unauthorized transmissions by him."

I don't ask how she knows this, but since her specialty is hacking computers, I'm not surprised she might be involved in the effort to safeguard the Lokarian systems.

"So, we're back to square one?" Layla asks. "The information is still in danger of getting into Skrum hands."

"I'm afraid so," Carter says.

Layla frowns. "I expected to fight the Skrum. I didn't expect to be dealing with traitors in our midst."

"Since we're a significant space flight from home, I guess we'd better bust our asses to track down the traitor," Elena says. "I, for one, have no intention of dying at an alien academy. "

Layla squares her shoulders. "Same." She sweeps her gaze across the room. "I know no one here is involved. Other than that, as far as I'm concerned, everyone at this academy is a suspect."

"My thoughts exactly." Carter jams his hands in the pockets of his uniform pants. "I'm afraid we've stumbled into something dark going on within the Lokarian military."

"What branch are you again?" Elena asks, studying the clean-cut cadet.

"Naval intelligence."

Elena gives him a small smile and nod. "Just the kind of guy we need to unravel this."

"Hey," I scold. "Hands off my friend. I saw him first."

"Don't be greedy," Layla says. "You can only have one hot guy at a time, and I don't think you want us sharing Koran with you."

"Not exactly." As much as I like my new girlfriends, I don't like them *that* much.

Elena throws an arm around Carter. "I promise we'll return him in one piece. Or close to it."

Carter's eyebrows lift as the tall woman jostles him. "That's comforting."

"I hope you aren't forgetting that we still have classes," Autumn says. "And some of us need to put in some extra work to pass. Traitor or no traitor, I'm not failing stupid hand-to-hand combat."

"She's right." I put a hand on Autumn's shoulder. "The whole reason we were sent here was to prepare us for the upcoming war with the Skrum. We can't ignore our classes, since we're learning stuff we're going to need."

Carter nods grimly. "Let's just hope the Skrum don't bring the war here to the academy."

CHAPTER THIRTY-ONE

Koran

I run my hands over the singed metal of the pod that Brooke had been riding. It's a miracle it's only blackened. I tap my knuckles on the hard steel that's now cool to the touch. No damage to its structure or strength. A coat of lacquer should be able to hide the discoloration.

I let out a breath, relief coursing through me that Brooke was not more damaged, as well. I'm still not sure how she managed to fly her way out of the explosion, but the thought of her being burned sends chills through me. For once, I'm grateful she's such a hotshot flier.

There are no sounds in my garage aside from my tapping on the pod hull. My classes were cancelled after word of the crash and explosion spread, and I spent most of day debriefing with Daryx.

As much as I like the Lokarian who recruited me, I hope I never have to sit through a grilling like that again. I'm only relieved I did not have any duplicity to confess related to my clan. Glatzor may be displeased that I gave him no information, but I'll deal with the repercussions of that later, if I ever rejoin my clan. Not only did Daryx commend me for discovering Vex's treachery, he offered me a permanent position as pod instructor.

I look around the dimly-lit space, the fading sunlight dappling the floor and sending long shadows stretching toward the wide opening onto the track. I would not mind staying here and teaching.

My mind returns to my prize pupil, and my heart trips in my chest. Even though I haven't known her long, it's hard to imagine being here without her. I chuckle as I think of what a pain in my ass she was at first, and then how quickly that changed.

"Is she salvageable?"

I don't need to turn to know that Brooke is walking up behind me, but I twist my head to watch her approach, regardless. She's no longer wearing her cadet uniform, but is in what I suspect are casual Earth clothes—snug black pants and a white, V-neck shirt tucked half in. My eyes drift to the hint of cleavage peeking out of her shirt, and she clears her throat.

"What?" I blink at her before remembering her question and glancing back at the damaged pod. "Nothing that can't be fixed."

She walks up next to me and put her small hand on the charred metal. "I owe this baby a lot for getting me out of that fire."

My throat is thick as I think back to the moment I saw the explosion engulf her. I'd never felt fear quite like that, and even now, my pulse skitters at the memory.

Clearing my throat roughly, I grab her by the waist and lift her onto the seat of the pod so that she's facing me.

"What do you think you're doing?" There isn't much genuine protest in her tone as she attempts to give me a stern look.

"Making it easier to do this." I wind an arm around her waist and tug her forward until her legs fall open and straddle me.

Her pupils flare, making her blue eyes dark. "You know I love being on a pod as much as the next girl, but don't you think there might be some better places we can think of?"

I nuzzle her neck. "Better places for what?"

She slaps at me playfully. "Don't play the big, dumb, pod rider with me. I know that's not you."

I nip at the skin on her neck, and she inhales sharply. "I thought you liked big."

"Have I mentioned how impossible you are?"

"Mm-hmm. A few times. Have I mentioned how good you taste?"

She moans as I lick my way down her throat, my tongue tracing underneath the neckline of her shirt and across the soft mound of her breast. She arches into me and clutches my shoulders, letting her head fall back.

"So, you don't want me to fuck you on the back of a pod again?" I ask, looking up.

She mumbles something incoherent and breathy. I lift her off the pod and toss her over my shoulder, taking long strides across the garage.

"Wait, where are you taking me?" She pushes herself up with her arms braced against my back.

I slap her ass gently. "You said you wanted someplace better than the back of a pod."

She yelps. "You can't carry me across campus like this, Koran."

I push open the door to my workshop. "Who said anything about me letting you out of here?" I cross the room to where I've set up a bed and hung a fabric canopy around it. I spin and plop her down on it, and she bounces on the soft surface a few times. "Will this do?"

Brooke props herself up on her elbows and looks around.

She rubs her hands over the dark silky sheets, then gives me a wicked smile. "I don't even want to know how you set this up, or who saw you dragging a bed across campus, but it's perfect."

I lean down, my arms on either side of her as I lower my body onto hers. "Good, because if you're not in class, I expect you to be right here with me."

"Oh, yeah? Doing what exactly, Koran?"

"Riding my cock."

Her eyelids flutter. "Yes, sir." She licks her bottom lip. "You know how I hate to disobey my teacher."

———

Want a bonus sexy scene between Brooke & Koran? Turn the page and sign-up to get the bonus scene and be on my VIP Reader list!

———

Next up is in the series is REBEL, book 2 in the Alien Academy series (Layla's story)!

It was supposed to be one night.

One night with the gorgeous, broken, enigmatic explosives expert who makes me crazy.

The problem? Now I can't stop fantasizing about the way we self-combusted all over each other.

One-click REBEL Now>

Don't miss any book in the Alien Academy series:

Book 2: Rebel (Hope Hart)

Book 3: Reckless (Miranda Bridges)

Book 4: Ruthless (Kyra Snow)

———

Want to read more hot alien romance after the Alien Academy Series? Try the sexy Drexian Warriors.

She's been promised a dream wedding. The catch? She was abducted from Earth and her groom is a hot alien warrior with a bad attitude. He's a big shot commander used to being obeyed, but no way is she following HIS orders. Sparks will fly in TAMED!

One-click TAMED Now>

"This crazy hot tale of the alpha male alien and the spoiled little rich girl of Beverly Hills is a funny, steamy, and highly engaging introduction to Tana Stone's new series. I gotta have more of this!"-Amazon Reviewer

———

This book has been edited and proofed, but typos are like little gremlins that like to sneak in when we're not looking. If you spot a typo, please report it to: tana@tanastone.com
Thank you!!

Want to read more steaminess between Brooke and Koran? Sign up to be on my VIP Reader list, and I'll send you a hot bonus epilogue! Being on my list also gets you sneak peeks of future books and bonus scenes exclusive to my VIPs!

Click here to get it:

https://BookHip.com/CGWASP

PREVIEW OF TAMED: TRIBUTE BRIDES OF THE DREXIAN WARRIORS BOOK #1

This is the first chapter of another sci-fi alien warrior romance series by Tana Stone—this one set on a high-tech space station and featuring badass Drexian warriors in need of human brides. I hope you enjoy!

Chapter One

Dorn strode across the deck of his ship's bridge, his heavy boots echoing off the steel floor, and scanned the large window that doubled as a view screen. The enemy was in retreat—that was clear from the distant explosions lighting up the inky blackness. He balled his hands into large fists, pleased that his fleet had once again kept the Kronock from getting close to the solar system his people had vowed to protect. As a Drexian warrior, known for battle skill and fearlessness, it was more than his duty. It was his life's mission.

"Report," he said to his number two in command.

"Inferno Force has repelled them again. Minor damage to our ship's hull, but nothing slipped past our blockade."

Dorn grunted in response, breathing in the faint smoky smell from the hit they'd taken. He knew as long as he led the fleet, nothing would get through. Although they were far from the eight-planet system containing Earth, he and his warriors put their lives at risk each day to keep the viscous Kronock from invading the technologically outmatched planet.

"Rerouting power back from shields to environmental controls," one of his officers said, intently focused on the computer screen.

A steamy bridge was a small price to pay for stronger shields, but he'd welcome some fresh airflow. Dorn swiped a hand across his sweaty brow as he took in the thousands of stars laid out in front of him.

Even though the Drexians had been defending Earth for over thirty years, almost no one on the blue planet was aware they even existed. That was part of the deal. The heads of government with whom they'd made first contact had insisted that discretion be the cornerstone of the arrangement. They'd thought telling humans about the existence of aliens—one warmongering species intent on invasion and one warrior race determined to stop the other—would create chaos and mass hysteria. So a secret agreement was forged that only a handful of Earthlings knew about.

"They don't even think life exists outside their world," Dorn said under his breath, lost in thought. "Arrogant fools."

"Come again, Commander?" the nearest deck officer asked, swiveling around in his chair and away from the monitor in front of him.

Dorn cleared his throat. "Nothing. Just glad the Kronock are on the run again. Good work, warriors."

"Yes, sir." The officer nodded and spun back around.

Dorn cast his eyes across the bridge at the Drexians all busy with their assigned tasks. Each wore dark uniform pants, and sleeveless shirts that pulled tight across their arms, exposing myriad tattoos and scars. Their faces were intense and focused on the battle, glowing with a sheen of sweat. The Drexians who signed up to serve in the Inferno Force and defend against the Kronock on the border of enemy territory—called the outskirts —were rougher than your average soldier.

Being so far away from the rest of the fleet, however, their rules were more relaxed. Dorn cultivated a fight hard, play hard mentality among his crew, and he lived it himself. Disagreements were settled with hand-to-hand combat, and he'd tasted blood—courtesy of his crewmates—more than once. He knew the Drexian High Command would not be pleased to see a bridge full of soldiers not in full uniform, but when he looked at the battle-scarred warriors, Dorn's chest swelled with pride. His eyes flicked to his own intricate, black tattoos stretching down one bicep--stylized swirls and a shield marking him as Inferno Force. He and his warriors would never let the Kronock through.

Pride morphed into anger as the thought of his enemy took hold. Violent and concerned only with exploiting other species, the gray-scaled warmongers wanted nothing more than to enslave and destroy. Even though they were technologically superior to humans, Kronock weaponry still hadn't been able to defeat the sheer firepower and sophisticated tech of the Drexian forces, which was why his people chased the monsters all over the galaxy to prevent them from invading weaker planets. It was how they'd discovered Earth in the first place. He knew many felt it had been a lucky day for both races.

Dorn spun on his heel and walked to the illuminated star chart that took up one wall of the bridge and traced the history of the war. He dragged a callused finger from the blue dot that represented the Drexian home world across light years to the small solar system so valuable to his people. He tapped the map, and his finger made the screen shimmer with ripples of color.

The small, blue planet looked tiny and insignificant, thought Dorn. In many ways it was. The planet was overpopulated, and was systematically destroying its own ecosystem, yet they had not achieved light speed, jump capability, or the ability to establish colonies off world. Normally, a planet such as that would not warrant a steady and devoted defense. In the past, the Drexians had relocated alien species that had been targeted by the Kronock, or had assimilated them into their society.

But Earth was different. Earth females were compatible with Drexian males. Some of them, at least. About half of the female population, according to Drexian scientists. This was why his fleet fought for them. This was why the human governments made the deal—the deal that traded protection of Earth for females.

Dorn turned from the star chart and watched his warriors move with practiced efficiency on the bridge. If there had been no deal, his crew would not be where it was. Not that Dorn minded fighting. None of them did, but sometimes he wondered if it would ever end.

After the initial Kronock incursion of the eight-planet solar system—when they'd reached within firing range of Earth before the Drexians had intervened and beaten them back—the enemy had sent a steady stream of ships to their border, but Dorn thought it was more to make sure the Drexians were still holding their blockade in place, than an actual attempt at invasion. The defense forces protecting Earth hadn't come face-to-face with a Kronock in over thirty years, and although Dorn's stomach turned at the thought of the huge scaly creatures with elongated, hairless heads his warrior father had told tales about, he couldn't help feeling that he was fighting a faceless enemy.

Keep on coming, he thought to himself as he watched his ship target a retreating Kronock ship and fire. Faceless or not, we'll beat you every time.

"The last Kronock ship has been pushed back, sir," his second in command said, looking over his shoulder from where he leaned against a low console.

"Are all our fighter pilots back?" Dorn asked.

His second glanced down at the console. "Last one just reported in. No losses."

He let out a breath, relieved that his team had suffered no casualties. He couldn't afford to lose any warriors. Correction, the Drexian race couldn't afford to lose any warriors.

As the last of the Kronock ships disappeared from view, Dorn's shoulders relaxed and he rubbed a hand across his jaw, feeling the day's worth of stubble he preferred. He had no problem defending Earth; battling the Kronock was in his blood and made him feel alive. However, he had no need or desire for an Earthling mate. Or a mate at all. His fellow Drexians could claim his share of the bounty for him.

"Fall back to our defensive orbit," he said, dragging a hand through the dark hair he'd let grow out and fall around his ears.

It wasn't that he found the Earth females repulsive. Aside from being small enough for him to break in two, they resembled Drexians in many ways. Bipedal mammals, they only lacked a foot or two in height, nodes along their spines, and a third breast, but he'd heard his Drexian brethren say that what the breasts lacked in quantity they made up for in softness. He'd often imagined what these famously soft breasts felt like, and even now his cock strained against his leg at the thought, and the hard nodes along his spine heated.

"Commander, you have an incoming transmission," his communications officer said, looking up from the blinking control panel.

"Transmit," Dorn said, glad for the interruption that had taken his mind off the Earth women and their curious breasts he'd never see.

The officer tilted his head. "It's on a secure line. From High Command."

Dorn sighed. "I'll take it in my strategy room."

He walked off the bridge and into an adjoining room where star charts and battle plans were strewn across a large, round table. Despite their technological sophistication, Dorn preferred mapping his strategy on paper. Drawing lines and charting intercept points helped him think clearly.

He took a seat across from the single display screen and tapped a button by the chair to start the transmission. The screen crackled to life, and a familiar face looked at him from across the galaxy. With bronze skin and vivid green eyes almost identical to his own, the man in the High Command uniform on the monitor grinned when he saw him. If Dorn's hair had been a lighter shade of brown and cut short, and one of his arms not covered with a dark swirl of tattoos, it might have been difficult to tell the two apart.

Dorn shook his head and tried not to smile himself. "I should have known it would be you. Nothing better to do than bother me in the middle of a battle?"

"Is that any way to greet your older brother?" The Drexian gave him a half grin. "Besides, I know you won your battle, and the Kronock are in full retreat."

Leave it to Kax to monitor his fleet. Once an older brother, always an older brother. Despite his twinge of annoyance, Dorn was glad to see his brother on screen. The two had always been close, and being so far from him was his one regret about commanding his battleship on the outskirts. Since Kax had left military intelligence and taken their father's seat at High Command, he rarely ventured to the edge of the defensive blockade anymore.

"You manage to get your information quickly," Dorn said, pushing a long sweaty strand of hair off his forehead. "We only just repelled the last of the ships."

Kax's smile faltered, and he took a breath. "Then now is the perfect time."

Dorn sat forward, resting his elbows on the table in front of him. He knew his brother's tell. Kax nervously rubbed his hands together, and an alarm bell sounded in the deep recesses of Dorn's brain. "The perfect time for what?"

"You're being recalled to High Command," his brother continued. "Well, more specifically, to the Boat."

The Boat? Dorn's mouth went dry. Why was he needed there? The massive space station—officially dubbed the Love Boat and called the Boat for short—had been built to accommodate and orient the Earth brides who were taken from the planet. It sat behind one of the moons of Saturn, hidden from view and space probes, not that those were as much of an issue since humans had stopped focusing resources on space exploration.

"I don't understand." Dorn tried to keep the panic from his voice.

"You will when you get here."

Dorn scowled at the screen. A typical answer from his brother. Did he always have to be so damned secretive? It wasn't like he was still an intelligence officer.

Kax shook his head. "I know how you feel about the Boat, but I hope you can put your issues aside."

"I don't have issues," Dorn said, hating the fact that he sounded like a petulant child. His older brother always did this to him. Put him on the defensive. Got him riled up.

"You think Earthlings are inferior."

Dorn shrugged. "They are. They've used their technology to strip their own planet bare. They're the only creatures I've ever seen willfully destroy their own habitat in this manner."

"Maybe," Kax said. "But regardless, of all the species we encountered on our search, they're the only ones who were biologically compatible."

Dorn grunted. "I know all that. The original DNA strand that managed to spread itself across the galaxy or something."

Kax angled his head at him. "You never did pay attention when it came to science, but yes, we do share common DNA with the humans. Otherwise we would not look so similar, or be able to successfully mate."

Of course, if the Drexians hadn't stopped producing females, they wouldn't have needed to search out other compatible species for mating, thought Dorn. But generations of war and defending weaker planets from invaders had depleted their population, and done something to their ability to create females. Almost none had been born in a generation.

"And these compatible beings still haven't figured out that we're taking females?"

Kax looked affronted. "You act like we're stealing them. You know very well that this is all done with the full permission of the Earth governments."

"Only because they had no choice," Dorn said. "Once they realized how technologically superior we are and were shown what the Kronock do to planets they invade, they had to agree to our terms, didn't they?"

Kax leaned back and blew out a long breath. "You make it sound like we blackmailed them. It's been a good deal for the humans. We protect Earth and keep the people from discovering about us and the possibility of an alien invasion."

"And they let us take their inferior two-breasted females for mates."

"Only a select few," Kax said. "You will not think them so inferior when you see them."

"I have no need to see them," Dorn insisted. "Besides, I'm busy tracking some unusual Kronock movements. I can't leave."

Kax pressed his brows together. "Unusual? In what way?"

Dorn gave a brusque shake of his hread. "It's hard to explain. I've spent years engaging our enemy, but lately they seem to be testing us more than actually trying to win."

"Why would they do that?" his brother asked.

Dorn didn't want to give voice to what he secretly feared. It was alarmist, and he had no proof, but he felt like the Kronock were waiting to spring something on them. Something big. "I can't say for sure."

"You can share your findings with the station's captain and the High Command when you arrive. I'm transmitting your official summons to the Boat."

Dorn scowled. He had never been there, had never had any reason to go there, but he'd heard it was a holographic wonderland meant to replicate everything most appealing about betrothal. Designers to create wedding gowns, jewelers to deck them out in gemstones, and exact recreations of some of Earth's most desirable locations. The theory was that if you enticed the females with enough bells and whistles for their marriages, they'd be less upset to be snatched from Earth and mated to an alien. From what he'd heard it worked reasonably well. It helped that they only took women who had no family connections and little reason to stay on Earth.

Dorn tried to imagine why he'd be needed on the Boat as he studied his brother's face. He'd never submitted an application for a bride and never intended to. "I'd rather be thrown in the brig."

His brother leaned back in his chair and grinned again, this time, followed by a throaty laugh. "You haven't changed a bit, brother. That's exactly what I thought you'd say."

To keep reading TAMED, click HERE

ALSO BY TANA STONE

Raider Warlords of the Vandar Series:

POSSESSED

PLUNDERED

Alien Academy Series:

ROGUE

The Tribute Brides of the Drexian Warriors Series:

TAMED (also available in AUDIO)

SEIZED (also available in AUDIO)

EXPOSED (also available in AUDIO)

RANSOMED (also available in AUDIO)

FORBIDDEN (also available in AUDIO)

BOUND

JINGLED (A Holiday Novella)

CRAVED

STOLEN

SCARRED

The Barbarians of the Sand Planet Series:

BOUNTY (also available in AUDIO)

CAPTIVE (also available in AUDIO)

TORMENT

TRIBUTE

SAVAGE

CLAIM

TANA STONE books available as audiobooks!

BARBARIANS OF THE SAND PLANET

BOUNTY on AUDIBLE

CAPTIVE on AUDIBLE

TRIBUTE BRIDES OF THE DREXIAN WARRIORS

TAMED on AUDIBLE

SEIZED on AUDIBLE

EXPOSED on AUDIBLE

RANSOMED on AUDIBLE

FORBIDDEN on AUDIBLE

ABOUT THE AUTHOR

Tana Stone is a bestselling sci-fi romance author who loves sexy aliens and independent heroines. Her favorite superhero is Thor (with Aquaman a close second because, well, Jason Momoa), her favorite dessert is key lime pie (okay, fine, *all* pie), and she loves Star Wars and Star Trek equally. She still laments the loss of *Firefly*.

She has one husband, two teenagers, and two neurotic cats. She sometimes wishes she could teleport to a holographic space station like the one in her tribute brides series (or maybe vacation at the oasis with the sand planet barbarians). :-)

She loves hearing from readers! Email her any questions or comments at tana@tanastone.com.

Want to hang out with Tana in her private Facebook group? Join on all the fun at: https://www.facebook.com/groups/tanastonestributes/

facebook.com/tanastoneauthor
instagram.com/tanastoneauthor
bookbub.com/authors/tana-stone